探险记

英国 Vampire Squid Productions 有限公司 | 著绘　　海豚传媒 | 编译

大洋猪

长江出版传媒 | 长江少年儿童出版社

图书在版编目（CIP）数据

大洋猪 / 英国 Vampire Squid Productions 有限公司著绘；海豚传媒编译 . -- 武汉：长江少年儿童出版社，2017.3
（海底小纵队探险记）
ISBN 978-7-5560-5547-0

Ⅰ . ①大… Ⅱ . ①英… ②海… Ⅲ . ①儿童故事—图画故事—英国—现代 Ⅳ . ① I561.85

中国版本图书馆 CIP 数据核字 (2016) 第 269700 号
著作权合同登记号：图字 17-2015-212

大洋猪

英国 Vampire Squid Productions 有限公司 / 著绘
海豚传媒 / 编译
责任编辑 / 傅一新　佟一　王炯
装帧设计 / 陈惠豪　美术编辑　刘菲
出版发行 / 长江少年儿童出版社
经　　销 / 全国新华书店
印　　刷 / 深圳当纳利印刷有限公司
开　　本 / 889×1194　1/20　5印张
版　　次 / 2017年6月第1版第3次印刷
书　　号 / ISBN 978-7-5560-5547-0
定　　价 / 16.80元

策　　划 / 海豚传媒股份有限公司（17061039）
网　　址 / www.dolphinmedia.cn　　邮　箱 / dolphinmedia@vip.163.com
阅读咨询热线 / 027-87391723　销售热线 / 027-87396822
海豚传媒常年法律顾问 / 湖北珞珈律师事务所　王清　027-68754966-227

本故事由英国Vampire Squid Productions 有限公司出品的动画节目所衍生，OCTONAUTS动画由Meomi公司的原创故事改编。
中国版权运营：北京万方幸星数码科技有限公司 授权热线：（北京）010-64381191

生命因探索而精彩

这是一部昭示生命美学与生态和谐的海洋童话，

这是一首承载生活教育与生存哲学的梦幻诗篇。

神秘浩瀚的海底世界，

能让孩子窥见物种诞生和四季交替，感受大自然生生不息的美感与力度；

引导他们关爱生命，关注生态平衡与绿色环保的重大现实。

惊险刺激的探险旅途，

能让孩子在因缘际会中，感知生活的缤纷底色与不可预知的精彩；

引领他们构建自我知识与品格系统，充盈成长的内驱力。

每一次完美的出发，

都是对生命的勇敢探索，更是对生活的热情礼赞！

人物档案

巴克队长

Captain Barnacles

巴克是一只北极熊，他是读解地图和图表的专家，探索未知海域和发现未知海洋生物是他保持旺盛精力的法宝。他勇敢、沉着、冷静，是小纵队引以为傲、值得信赖的队长，他的果敢决策激励着每一位成员。

呱唧

Kwazii

呱唧是一只冲动的橘色小猫，有过一段神秘的海盗生涯。他性格豪放，常常会讲起自己曾经的海盗经历。呱唧热爱探险，将探险家精神展现得淋漓尽致。虽然他是只猫咪，但他从不吃鱼哟！

皮医生

Peso

皮医生是一只可爱的企鹅。他是小纵队的医生，如果有人受伤，需要救治，他会全力以赴。他的勇气来自一颗关爱别人的心，无论是大型海洋动物还是小小浮游生物，都很喜欢皮医生。

谢灵通

Shellington

谢灵通是一只海獭，随身携带着一个用来观察生物的放大镜。他博学多识，无所不知，常常能发现队友们所忽略的关键细节。不过，他有时候容易分心，常常被新鲜事物所吸引。

达西西

Dashi

达西西是一只腊肠狗，她是小纵队的官方摄影师。她拍摄的影像是海底小纵队资料库中必不可少的一部分，而且还纳入了章鱼堡电脑系统的档案中。

突突兔

Tweak

突突兔是小纵队的机械工程师，负责维护和保养小纵队所有的交通工具。为了小纵队的某项特殊任务，突突兔还要对部分机械进行改造。她还热衷于发明一些新奇的东西，这些发明有时能派上大用场。

小萝卜

Tunip

小萝卜和其他六只植物鱼是小纵队的厨师，负责小纵队全体成员的饮食等家政服务，还管理着章鱼堡的花园。植物鱼们有自己独特的语言，这种语言只有谢灵通才能听得懂。

章教授

Professor Inkling

章教授是一只小飞象章鱼，左眼戴着单片眼镜，很爱读书，见多识广。当队员们出去执行任务的时候，他会待在基地负责联络工作。

🐙 目录 CONTENTS

海底小纵队与后颌鱼

洋流就要来了，巴克队长正拿着扩音器对海洋生物们喊话："海里的动植物们，注意啦！今天洋流格外强大，所以千万要小心！找安全的地方待着！"生物们听到后立刻分散开来，去寻找避难所。

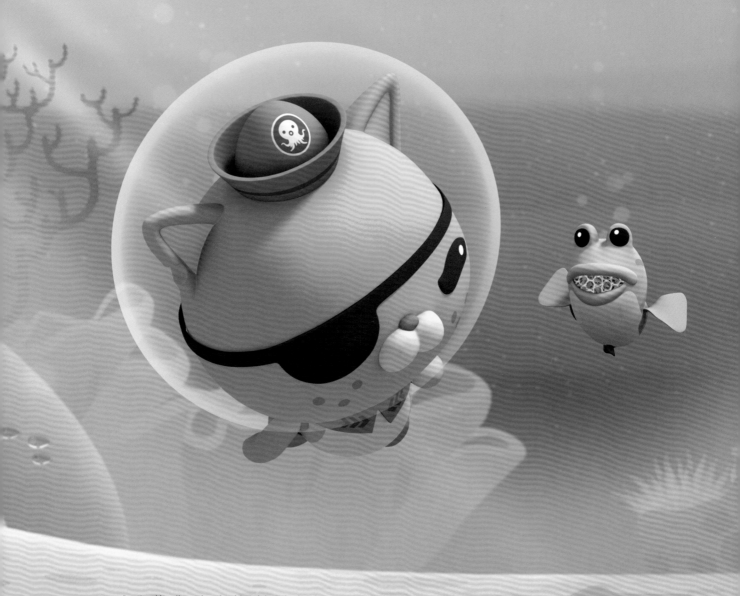

guā jī lái dào yì zhī hòu hé yú shēn biān　wèn dào　　wèi　péng you　　nǐ tīng dào tōng zhī le ma
呱唧来到一只后颌鱼身边，问道："喂，朋友！你听到通知了吗？"

hòu hé yú biān yóu biān huí dá　　kě tā de zuǐ li sì hū hán zhe shén me dōng xi　　guā jī gēn běn
后颌鱼边游边回答，可他的嘴里似乎含着什么东西，呱唧根本

tīng bù dǒng tā zài shuō shén me　　　yú shì jiàn yì tā fàng màn yǔ sù
听不懂他在说什么，于是建议他放慢语速。

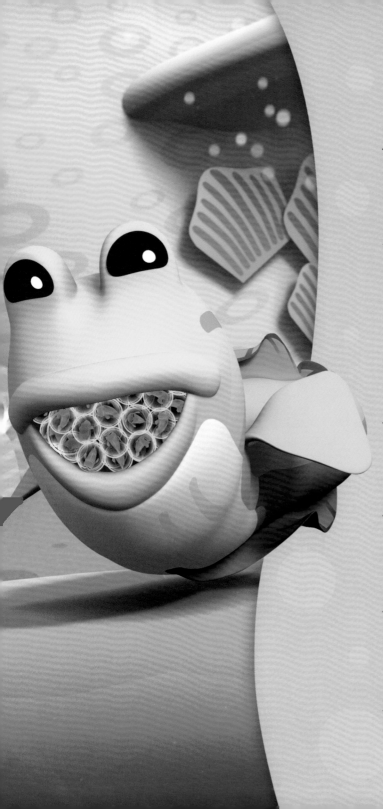

后颌鱼费劲地讲道："我说我叫吉米，我要回家，回我的洞穴，我的洞穴就是这儿，但我嘴里却装满了……"

"鱼卵！噢！我的鱼卵掉了！"几个小东西从他的嘴里掉了出来，后颌鱼连忙将它们重新含进了嘴里。

突然，洋流来了，后颌鱼被刮倒在地，几颗鱼卵又从他的嘴里掉了出来，被洋流卷走了，后颌鱼很着急。这时，巴克队长和皮医生赶了过来，安抚了后颌鱼后，巴克队长启动了章鱼警报。

"海底小纵队，

去发射台！”

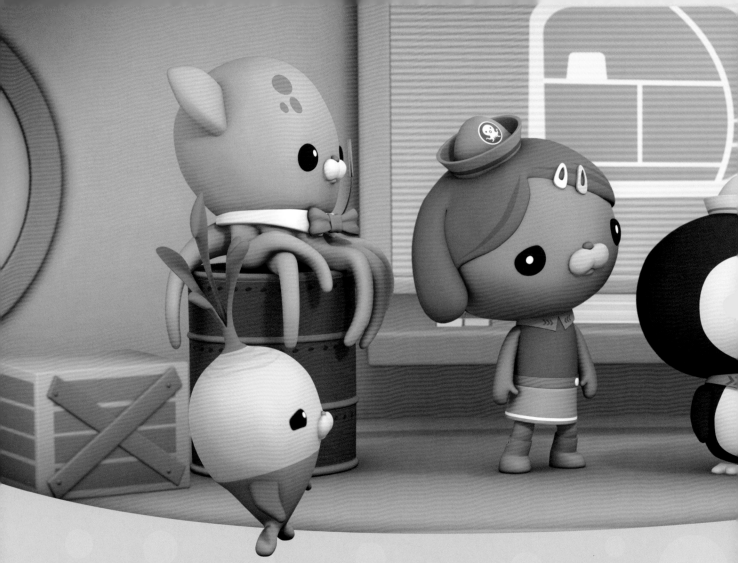

大家到齐后，巴克队长说道："洋流将十颗后颌鱼的鱼卵卷走了，我们要找到它们并送回它们爸爸的嘴里。"

突突兔听了十分好奇，谢灵通解释道："鱼卵需要一直待在后颌鱼爸爸的嘴里，直到孵化出来。"

巴克队长让达西西启动了洋流追踪仪。"洋流沿着峭壁，
越过了间歇泉，穿过了山谷……"达西西汇报道。

巴克队长、呱唧和皮医生分头寻找鱼卵，谢灵通和后颌鱼
待在洞穴里，而达西西则继续追踪洋流。小萝卜也加入了行动。

chū fā qián bā kè duì zhǎng dān yōu de shuō nà xiē yú luǎn tài xiǎo tài róu ruò le
出发前，巴克队长担忧地说："那些鱼卵太小太柔弱了……"

tū tū tù mǎ shàng ná chū le tā de mì mì wǔ qì yú luǎn shōu jí qì tā men néng shōu jí
突突兔马上拿出了她的秘密武器——鱼卵收集器，它们能收集

yú luǎn bìng bǎo zhèng tā men de ān quán tā jiāng yú luǎn shōu jí qì fēn gěi le bā kè duì zhǎng pí yī shēng
鱼卵并保证它们的安全。她将鱼卵收集器分给了巴克队长、皮医生

hé guā jī
和呱唧。

突突兔又将背包递给了他们，兴奋地说："我把气罐改装成了喷射背包，只要按一下这个按钮，你们就会强力加速，逆流而上啦。"

说完，突突兔开启了章鱼堡的舱门，巴克队长、呱唧和皮医生分别驾驶着灯笼鱼艇、虎鲨艇和孔雀鱼艇出发了。

"皮医生，你沿着峭壁找；呱唧，你顺着间歇泉找；我在山谷这里找！"巴克队长安排好后，大家开始分头行动。

皮医生很快就在峭壁那里找到了两颗鱼卵。

接着，他发现了第三颗鱼卵，可是鱼卵后面有一只魔鬼鱼。皮医生急坏了，"魔鬼鱼看到什么就吃什么！"

皮医生加速前进，赶在魔鬼鱼张嘴之前，收集到了这颗鱼卵。

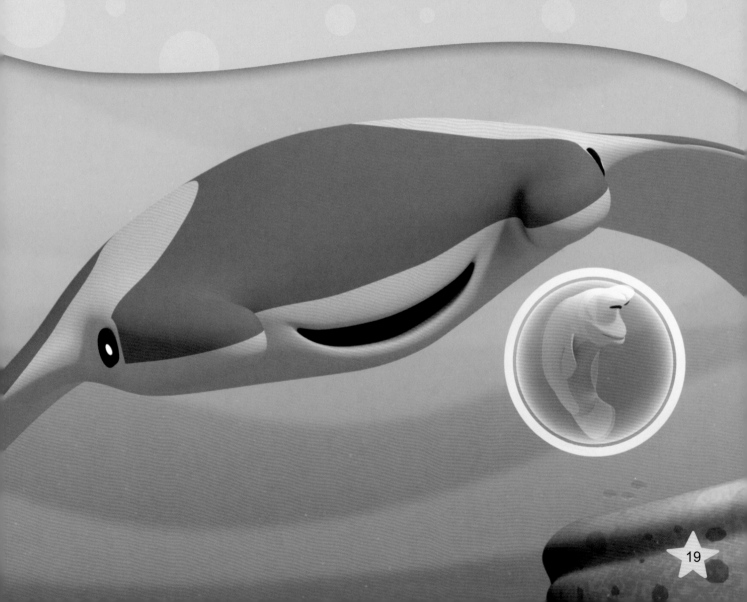

此时，在后颌鱼的洞口，小萝卜高兴地告诉谢灵通，他找到了鱼卵。令人失望的是，他把鹅卵石当成了鱼卵，谢灵通只好鼓励他继续寻找。

这时，皮医生驾驶着孔雀鱼艇过来了，他从舰艇里出来，游到后颌鱼面前，对他说道："给你！三颗鱼卵，完好无损。"说着，皮医生将鱼卵一一喷射到后颌鱼的嘴里。

谢灵通将情况汇报给了巴克队长，现在还剩下七颗鱼卵。

21

另一边，呱唧已经到了间歇泉附近，他驾驶着虎鲨艇，在间歇泉间来回穿梭。受水流的影响，虎鲨艇有些失控。不一会儿，虎鲨艇终于冲出来，到了平静的水域。

guā jī gāng tíng xià lái　jiù shōu jí dào liǎng kē yú luǎn　zài jiàn xiē quán
呱唧刚停下来，就收集到两颗鱼卵。在间歇泉

de pēn kǒu tā fā xiàn le lìng yì kē yú luǎn　tā lì kè chōng guò qù　dàn
的喷口他发现了另一颗鱼卵，他立刻冲过去，但

pēn kǒu de shuǐ liú bǎ yú luǎn chōng xiàng le kōng zhōng　guā jī lián máng qǐ dòng pēn
喷口的水流把鱼卵冲向了空中。呱唧连忙启动喷

shè bēi bāo　téng kōng yuè qǐ　chéng gōng shōu jí dào le yú luǎn
射背包，腾空跃起，成功收集到了鱼卵。

23

"鱼卵送来啦，张嘴！"呱唧很快来到后
领鱼身边，将鱼卵喷射进他的嘴里。

谢灵通立刻向巴克队长汇报情况："队长，我
们又发现了三颗鱼卵。"

"我这儿也发现两颗。"巴克队长拿出计数器，
说道，"加在一起有八颗了，继续找另外两颗。"

巴克队长正说着话，突然一块石头砸下
来，幸好他躲过了，现在收集鱼卵越来越困难。

bā kè duì zhǎng cóng jiàn tǐng zhōng chū lai　　xiǎo xīn de bì kāi luò xià de yí kuài yòu yí kuài shí tou
巴克队长从舰艇中出来，小心地避开落下的一块又一块石头，

zhōng yú fā xiàn bìng chéng gōng shōu jí dào le dì jiǔ kē yú luǎn
终于发现并成功收集到了第九颗鱼卵！

wǒ zhǎo dào sān kē　　ān rán wú yàng　　bā kè duì zhǎng lái dào hòu hé yú shēn biān　　jiāng yú luǎn
"我找到三颗，安然无恙。"巴克队长来到后颌鱼身边，将鱼卵

^{pēn shè jìn tā de zuǐ li} ^{jiǔ kē le} ^{hái chà yì kē}
喷射进他的嘴里，"九颗了……还差一颗。"

^{hòu hé yú shāng xīn de shuō zhe shén me} ^{xiè líng tōng fān yì dào} ^{tā jiào xiǎo jí mǐ} ^{shì kē}
后颌鱼伤心地说着什么，谢灵通翻译道："它叫小吉米，是颗

^{kě ài} ^{yǒng gǎn bìng yǒu zhe mào xiǎn xì bāo de yú luǎn}
可爱、勇敢并有着冒险细胞的鱼卵。"

^{bā kè duì zhǎng lì kè hū jiào dá xī xī} ^{gào su tā} ^{hái yǒu yì kē yú luǎn méi zhǎo dào} ^{tā}
巴克队长立刻呼叫达西西，告诉她："还有一颗鱼卵没找到，它

^{de míng zi jiào xiǎo jí mǐ}
的名字叫小吉米。"

27

达西西看了看洋流的踪迹图，说道："最后那颗鱼卵可能还被困在洋流里，越过了山谷，朝开阔海域的方向去了。"巴克队长、呱唧和皮医生马上出发，跟上洋流，很快就发现了小吉米。

可是这股洋流太强大了，鱼卵收集器根本无法发挥作用。巴克队长试图用手去抓，鱼卵太滑，弹了出去，落到了大蛤蜊的壳上。

呱唧刚要抓，大蛤蜊张开外壳，鱼卵又被弹走了，被三只柠檬鲨包围起来。

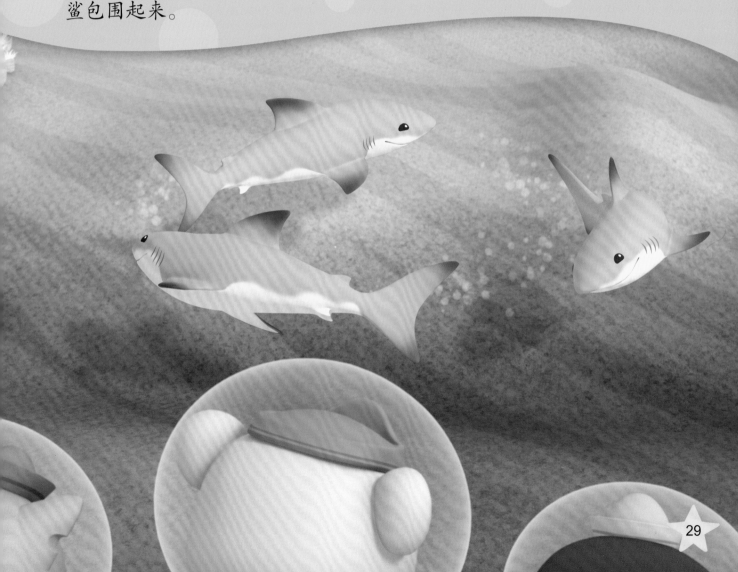

wǒ néng duì fu tā men　　duì zhǎng　　　guā jī shuō zhe jiù xiǎng chōng chu qu　　bā kè
"我能对付他们，队长！"呱唧说着就想冲出去。巴克

duì zhǎng lián máng lā zhù le tā　　jiāo dài dào　　　guā jī　　xiǎo xīn　　bù néng ràng tā men fā
队长连忙拉住了他，交代道："呱唧，小心！不能让他们发

xiàn wǒ men　　yóu dào tā men xià miàn qù
现我们，游到他们下面去。"

zūn mìng　　duì zhǎng　　　guā jī dī shēng
"遵命，队长！"呱唧低声

huí yìng dào　　qiāo qiāo liū dào le níng méng shā xià
回应道，悄悄溜到了柠檬鲨下

fāng　　shōu jí dào le yú luǎn
方，收集到了鱼卵。

níng méng shā mǎ shàng jiù fā xiàn le tā
柠檬鲨马上就发现了他，

wèi nà jiā huo dàng zuò líng shí yīng gāi tǐng hǎo chī
"喂！那家伙当作零食应该挺好吃

de yǎn kàn zhe níng méng shā zhuī le guò lái
的！"眼看着柠檬鲨追了过来，

guā jī zhǐ hǎo bǎ yú luǎn shōu jí qì rēng gěi pí yī
呱唧只好把鱼卵收集器扔给皮医

shēng yú luǎn shōu jí qì zài tā men shǒu zhōng lái
生……鱼卵收集器在他们手中来

huí chuán dì
回传递。

现在鱼卵收集器又回到了呱唧手中，而柠檬鲨步步紧逼，呱唧迫不得已只好将鱼卵收集器扔给了柠檬鲨。

呱唧则趁机跑到了巴克队长和皮医生面前，巴克队长大喊道："呱唧，你疯了吗？"

bié dān xīn　guā jī zhāng kāi shǒu　jiě shì dào　xiǎo jí mǐ wán hǎo wú sǔn

"别担心。"呱唧张开手，解释道，"小吉米完好无损。"

yuán lái guā jī zài rēng yú luǎn shōu jí qì zhī qián　yǐ jīng xiān jiāng yú luǎn pēn shè dào le zì jǐ shǒu li

原来呱唧在扔鱼卵收集器之前，已经先将鱼卵喷射到了自己手里。

zài jiàn le　níng méng shā　guā jī dà hǎn zhe　hé duì yuán men yì qǐ lí kāi le zhè lǐ

"再见了！柠檬鲨！"呱唧大喊着，和队员们一起离开了这里。

他们来到了后颌鱼的身边，呱唧高兴地伸出手，可是他手里的鱼卵不见了。大家连忙低头寻找，这时，小萝卜拿来一个东西，谢灵通定睛一看，"是颗鱼卵！"

小萝卜将鱼卵放进了后颌鱼的嘴里，十颗鱼卵终于全部找到了。

很快，鱼卵就孵出来了。后颌鱼又叽里咕噜说了一阵，开始埋头啃泥沙，呱唧很疑惑。谢灵通说道："我想他是说他在用嘴刨洞。"

"我说的正是这个！"

后颌鱼回应道。大家听了哈哈大笑起来。

欢迎进入本期海底报告，这次我们要介绍的是**后颌鱼**！

后颌鱼真有办法

保护鱼卵不害怕

后颌鱼爸爸张开嘴

鱼卵统统都装下

它们嘴巴功能多

挖洞和筑窝，全靠大嘴巴

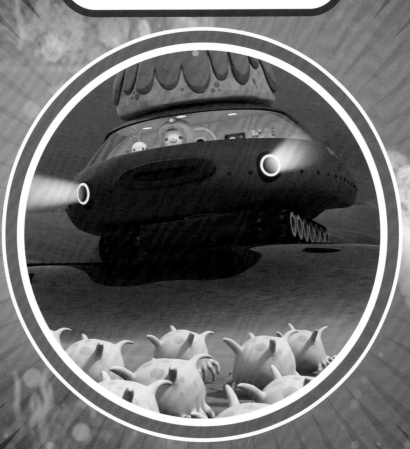

海底小纵队与大洋猪

zhāng yú bǎo zhèng jīng guò yí gè dà hǎi gōu　　hǎi dǐ xiǎo zòng duì yào zài hǎi gōu fù jìn zhǎo gè
章鱼堡正经过一个大海沟，海底小纵队要在海沟附近找个

ān quán de dì fang zhuó lù
安全的地方着陆。

wǒ de lǎo tiān yé ya　　　hǎi chuáng quán shì fěn hóng sè de　　kàn qǐ lai hái zài dǒu dòng
"我的老天爷呀！海床全是粉红色的，看起来还在抖动！"

guā jī jīng qí de xiān kāi yǎn zhào　　kàn zhe yǎn qián de jǐng xiàng
呱唧惊奇地掀开眼罩，看着眼前的景象。

xiè líng tōng　　nǐ zěn me kàn
"谢灵通，你怎么看？"

bā kè duì zhǎng zhǐ le zhǐ wài miàn
巴克队长指了指外面。

tài shén qí le　　duì zhǎng　　nà shì
"太神奇了，队长，那是

dà yáng zhū　　xiè líng tōng gěi dà jiā jiě shì
大洋猪。"谢灵通给大家解释，

dà yáng zhū shì shēn hǎi zhōng de dòng wù　　dàn
"大洋猪是深海中的动物，但

shì bú huì yóu yǒng　　tā men zhǐ huì yòng xiǎo
是不会游泳，他们只会用小

duǎn tuǐ zài hǎi chuáng shang sì chù zǒu dòng
短腿在海床上四处走动。"

tā men hǎo xiàng shì chòng zhe hǎi gōu qù de　　pí yī shēng guān chá zhe dà yáng zhū de fāng xiàng
"他们好像是冲着海沟去的。"皮医生观察着大洋猪的方向。

bù hǎo　rú guǒ tā men diào xia qu　kě jiù yóu bú shàng lái le　xiè líng tōng chōng dào xiǎn shì
"不好，如果他们掉下去，可就游不上来了。"谢灵通冲到显示

píng qián chá kàn mó nǐ tú xiàng　jīng hū dào
屏前查看模拟图像，惊呼道。

nà xià tou kě shēn zhe ne　huǒ ji　guā jī bǔ chōng shuō
"那下头可深着呢，伙计！"呱唧补充说。

hái bù zhǐ zhè yí gè wèn tí　　dà yáng zhū chī de shì cóng hǎi yáng biǎo miàn piāo luò de shí wù　　dàn
"还不止这一个问题！大洋猪吃的是从海洋表面漂落的食物。但

shì　　shí wù bù kě néng diào dào nà me shēn de dì fang　　xiè líng tōng shuō
是，食物不可能掉到那么深的地方。"谢灵通说。

bā kè duì zhǎng gǎn jǐn hào zhào dà jiā lái dào fā shè tái　　wǒ men bù néng ràng dà yáng zhū diào xia
巴克队长赶紧号召大家来到发射台，"我们不能让大洋猪掉下

qu　　zhǔn bèi jiàn tǐng　　suí hòu　　tā men jiù chū fā le
去，准备舰艇！"随后，他们就出发了。

41

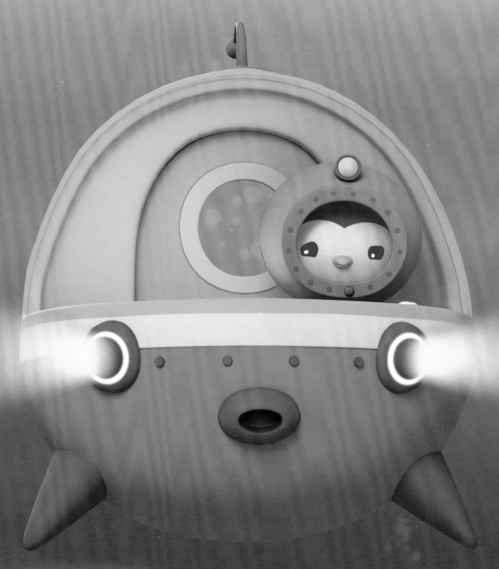

bù jiǔ，hǎi dǐ xiǎo zòng duì lái dào dà yáng zhū de qián fāng，bā kè duì zhǎng

不久，海底小纵队来到大洋猪的前方。巴克队长

shuō：qǐng lì kè wǎng huí zǒu，yīn wèi nǐ men de qián fāng shì

说："请立刻往回走，因为你们的前方是……"

"食物！"一只大洋猪马上接话。

大洋猪们根本不理会巴克队长，对于皮医生的提醒，他们也当作没听到。

谢灵通似乎明白过来了，他告诉队长，大洋猪应该是闻到了海沟对面的食物的味道，大洋猪的嗅觉很灵敏。

"那我们就找到吸引他们的东西，然后放到海沟的这边，来让他们吃。"巴克队长说。

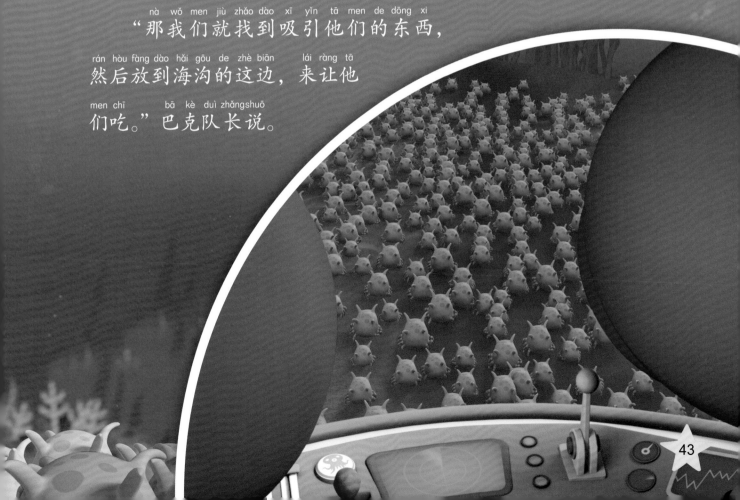

43

méi guò duō jiǔ　　 tā men jiù zhǎo dào le yí dà piàn nián nián de dōng
没过多久，他们就找到了一大片黏黏的东

xi　　xiè líng tōng gào su dà jiā　　zhè shì cóng hǎi
西。谢灵通告诉大家，这是从海

yáng biǎo miàn chén xia lai de fǔ làn hǎi zǎo
洋表面沉下来的腐烂海藻，

duì dà yáng zhū lái shuō　　shì jiàn kāng
对大洋猪来说，是健康

shí wù　　dàn shì bǎ zhè xiē shí
食物。但是把这些食

wù shōu jí qi lai　　xū yào hěn
物收集起来，需要很

cháng shí jiān
长时间。

44

这时候，皮医生传来消息："大洋猪离海沟越来越近了，必须抓紧时间。"

巴克队长想了想，说："尽快把这些东西装到舰艇上去，我想应该有办法转移他们的注意力。"

大家听了，立刻行动起来。

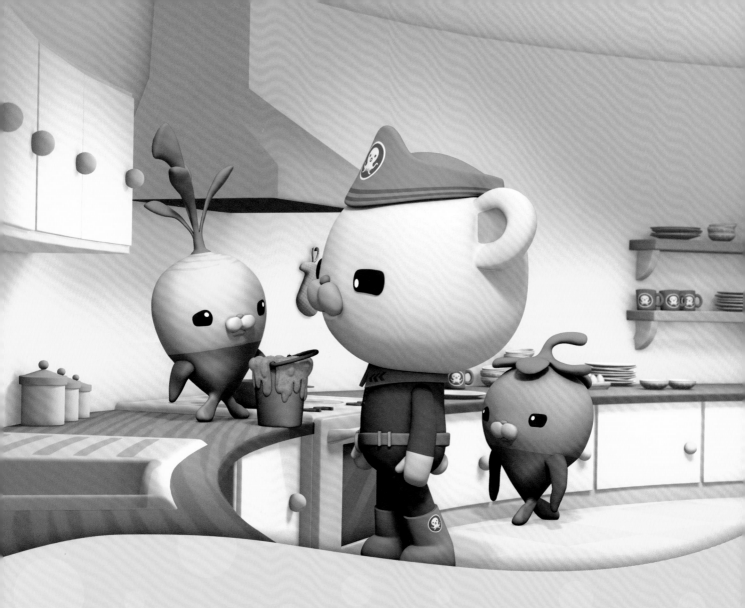

bā kè duì zhǎng zé huí dào zhāng yú bǎo　　bǎ yì tǒng nán wén de fǔ làn hǎi zǎo jiāo gěi zhí wù yú
巴克队长则回到章鱼堡，把一桶难闻的腐烂海藻交给植物鱼

men　shuō dào　　　nǐ men néng yòng zhè xiē hǎi zǎo　　wèi yì qún jī è de dà yáng zhū zuò yí dùn chāo jí nán
们，说道："你们能用这些海藻，为一群饥饿的大洋猪做一顿超级难

wén de shèng yàn ma　　ér qiě yào kuài
闻的盛宴吗？而且要快！"

zhí wù yú men mǎ shàng tóu rù dào le jǐn zhāng de gōng zuò zhōng
植物鱼们马上投入到了紧张的工作中。

hěn kuài shí wù jiù zuò hǎo le bā kè duì zhǎng bǐng zhù hū xī shuō dào xiǎo luó bo
很快，食物就做好了。巴克队长屏住呼吸说道："小萝卜，

zhè zhēn shì tài nán wén le hǎo yàng de dà yáng zhū men kěn dìng xǐ huan
这真是太难闻了！好样的，大洋猪们肯定喜欢！"

47

巴克队长将这个巨大的食物绑在马蹄蟹艇上，然后就出发了。

"队长，我没法继续阻止他们了！"皮医生发来求助信息。

"你也不需要了！"巴克队长已经快到了。

果然，大洋猪们闻到了巴克队长带过来的食物的味道，立刻调转了方向。

49

"食物……好吃……"大洋猪一边嘟哝着，一边成群结队地往马蹄蟹艇这边走。

皮医生被眼前的景象惊呆了，"我的小乖乖呀，他们往回走了！"

眼看着接近大洋猪了，巴克队长说道："就这样，小萝卜，停下！我要把这顿大餐给卸下来。"

巴克队长走出舰艇，拉动绳索。但食物掉下来一部分后，马蹄蟹艇陷落到了泥地里。队长立刻呼叫皮医生过来帮忙。

^{pí yī shēng hěn kuài gǎn dào le} ^{bā kè duì zhǎng jiāng shéng suǒ gù}
皮医生很快赶到了，巴克队长将绳索固

^{dìng zài le kǒng què yú tǐng shang}
定在了孔雀鱼艇上。

^{hǎo le} ^{pí yī shēng} ^{xī wàng nǐ de kǒng què yú tǐng néng gòu}
"好了，皮医生，希望你的孔雀鱼艇能够

^{chéng shòu zhù} ^{bā kè duì zhǎng shuō zhe} ^{yòu mìng lìng xiǎo luó bo} ^{quán}
承受住。"巴克队长说着，又命令小萝卜，"全

^{lì xiàng hòu lā}
力向后拉！"

^{xiǎo luó bo fèn lì jiāng mǎ tí xiè tǐng de cāo zuò gǎn wǎng hòu lā}
小萝卜奋力将马蹄蟹艇的操作杆往后拉，

^{yí bù xiǎo xīn bèi cāo zuò gǎn fǎn tán dào le cāo zuò tái shang} ^{bìng qiě chù}
一不小心被操作杆反弹到了操作台上，并且触

^{fā le yí gè qǐ dòng àn niǔ}
发了一个启动按钮。

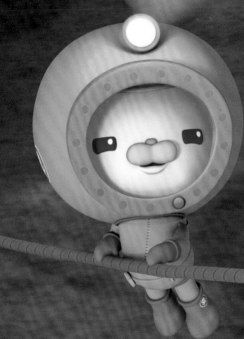

^{jié guǒ} ^{mǎ tí xiè tǐng de qián bàn bù}
结果，马蹄蟹艇的前半部

^{fen} ^{huá xiáng jī tuō lí gǔn lún} ^{dài zhe xiǎo}
分——滑翔机脱离滚轮，带着小

^{luó bo hé dà bù fen shí wù kuài sù wǎng qián shǐ qù}
萝卜和大部分食物快速往前驶去。

52

53

"小萝卜！"巴克队长和皮医生被这突然
发生的一切惊到了，他们异口同声地喊道。

失控的滑翔机不停地往前行驶，很快，它就落入了海沟。

然而更可怕的是，一部分大洋猪闻到滑翔机上食物的味道，追了过来，跟着滑翔机掉入了海沟。

"皮医生，快！"见此情景，巴克队长和皮医生分别驾驶着舰艇跟了上去。

"呱唧，小萝卜掉到海沟里了，现在你得马上去找他，快！"巴克队长呼叫呱唧，然后又吩咐其他队员，"其他人听好了，有些大洋猪也随着滑翔机走进了海沟里面，我们也要营救他们。"

"遵命，队长！"大家立刻停止手头的事情，驾驶着舰艇向海沟出发了。呱唧驾驶着虎鲨艇，很快发现了滑翔机。但是，滑翔机撞到海底后，被淹埋在了泥土下面，呱唧一下子失去了营救目标。

另一边，其他队员们正努力营救大洋猪。但是大洋猪数量多，而且目标分散，营救起来难度很大。

"队长，我们不能挨个儿救，时间已经来不及了！"突突兔焦急地说道。

"那就把他们赶到一起去。"巴克队长很快就想出了办法。

他们驾驶着舰艇，围着大洋者转圈，舰艇的运动带动了周围的水流，形成了漩涡，大猪随着漩涡旋转起来。

bā kè duì zhǎng yào pí yī shēng dǎ kāi kǒng què yú tǐng
巴克队长要皮医生打开孔雀鱼艇

de hòu bèi cāng　zài xià miàn jiē yìng　dà yáng zhū màn màn
的后备舱，在下面接应。大洋猪慢慢

de dōu luò zài le kǒng què yú tǐng de hòu bèi cāng li
地都落在了孔雀鱼艇的后备舱里。

gǎo dìng le　pí yī shēng gāo xìng de shuō dào
"搞定了！"皮医生高兴地说道，

tā dài zhe dà yáng zhū　hé dà huǒ er yì qǐ lí kāi le hǎi gōu
他带着大洋猪，和大伙儿一起离开了海沟。

dà yáng zhū dé jiù hòu　bā kè duì zhǎng kāi shǐ hū jiào guā jī
大洋猪得救后，巴克队长开始呼叫呱唧，

kàn dào xiǎo luó bo hé huá xiáng jī le ma
"看到小萝卜和滑翔机了吗？"

guā jī gào su duì zhǎng　　xiǎo luó bo bú jiàn le　　qǐng qiú zhī yuán

呱唧告诉队长："小萝卜不见了，请求支援！"

wǒ men xū yào de bù zhǐ shì zhī yuán   hái yào yí gè jì
"我们需要的不只是支援，还要一个计

huà   duì zhǎng shuō zhe zhuā zhù yì zhī dà yáng zhū   ér qiě   wǒ
划。"队长说着抓住一只大洋猪，"而且，我

xiǎng wǒ yǐ jīng yǒu bàn fǎ le
想我已经有办法了。"

duì zhǎng jiāng nà zhī dà yáng zhū fàng jìn jiàn tǐng li   hé pí yī
队长将那只大洋猪放进舰艇里，和皮医

shēng yì qǐ chū fā le
生一起出发了。

yuán lái   duì zhǎng shì xiǎng yòng huá xiáng jī
原来，队长是想用滑翔机

dǐng duān shí wù de wèi dào xī yǐn dà yáng zhū ràng
顶端食物的味道吸引大洋猪，让

dà yáng zhū dài tā men zhǎo dào xiǎo luó bo zhè ge
大洋猪带他们找到小萝卜。这个

fāng fǎ fēi cháng zòu xiào dà yáng zhū hěn kuài jiù zhǎo
方法非常奏效，大洋猪很快就找

dào le wèi dào de lái yuán
到了味道的来源。

dà jiā jiāng ní tǔ bā kāi
大家将泥土扒开，

guǒ rán kàn dào le xiǎo luó bo hái
果然看到了小萝卜，还

yǒu shī zōng de huá xiáng jī
有失踪的滑翔机。

63

接着，他们用虎鲨艇和孔
雀鱼艇将滑翔机拉出了海沟。

"谢谢你帮忙！没有你的
话，我们就真没办法了。"巴克
队长走出舰艇，对那只正在享
用美食的大洋猪说道。

"大家来吃个痛快吧！"达西西将之前收集到的食物全部发放给了大洋猪。

看到大洋猪们吃得如此享受，呱唧感叹道："他们真的超喜欢这个味道啊！"

"小萝卜才真是有苦难言呢！"巴克队长打趣道。大伙儿都笑了起来。

65

欢迎进入本期海底报告，这次我们要介绍的是**大洋猪**！

大洋猪们四处逛

它们住在海床上

依靠小腿慢慢爬

游泳技术不灵光

拱寻食物不停歇

找食用鼻子，嗅觉超级棒

海底小纵队与狮鬃水母

章鱼堡外，皮医生正在给一只叫狮宝的狮鬃水母检查身体。

皮医生绕着狮鬃水母从上往下，一圈圈游着，只听他一边游一边说道："很好，很好，都挺好的……"

"现在还有一个超级小的触手需要解开！这不会疼的。"

皮医生游到底部，发现了一点小问题。

"哈嚓嘿呀！"皮医生说道。很快，触手就解开了，他朝狮宝上方游去。

pí yī shēng　nǐ zhēn shì hǎi
"皮医生，你真是海

yáng zhōng zuì wěi dà de yī shēng le　hā hā
洋中最伟大的医生了！哈哈！

wǒ men lái gè yōng bào ba　shuō zhe　shī bǎo jiù
我们来个拥抱吧？"说着，狮宝就

yòng chù shǒu jiāng pí yī shēng lā dào le zì jǐ gēn qián
用触手将皮医生拉到了自己跟前。

pí yī shēng xià yì shí de jiào le yì shēng　hòu tuì
皮医生下意识地叫了一声，后退

le jǐ bù　shī bǎo gǎn dào hěn bào qiàn
了几步，狮宝感到很抱歉。

70

皮医生连忙安慰道："没事的，狮宝！我穿着防蜇服呢，而且你是一只狮鬃水母——你们一向都是这样的！"

"哈哈！你说得对！这样才能保护我自己和朋友们！"狮宝刚说完，几只船头鱼就从他的触手中游了出来。

不远处，一只狗鲨游了过来，狮宝继续说道："如果有大鱼胆敢打我朋友的主意，哼！我就给他点颜色看看！对不对？"

很快，狮宝就对游过来的狗鲨发起了攻击，狗鲨被刺得赶紧游向了另一边。

gǒu shā zǒu hòu　　yì zhī chuán tóu yú lián máng huí dá　　shuō de méi cuò　　shī bǎo
狗鲨走后，一只船头鱼连忙回答："说的没错，狮宝！"

xiàn zài wēi xiǎn yǐ jīng jiě chú le　　pí yī shēng xiào zhe duì dà jiā shuō dào　　nǐ men yǒu shuí xū
现在危险已经解除了，皮医生笑着对大家说道："你们有谁需

yào jiǎn chá shēn tǐ　　zài lái gè xiào liǎn tiē ne
要检查身体，再来个笑脸贴呢？"

wǒ　　wǒ　　wǒ　　　　chuán tóu yú men zhēng xiān kǒng hòu de shuō dào
"我、我、我……"船头鱼们争先恐后地说道。

73

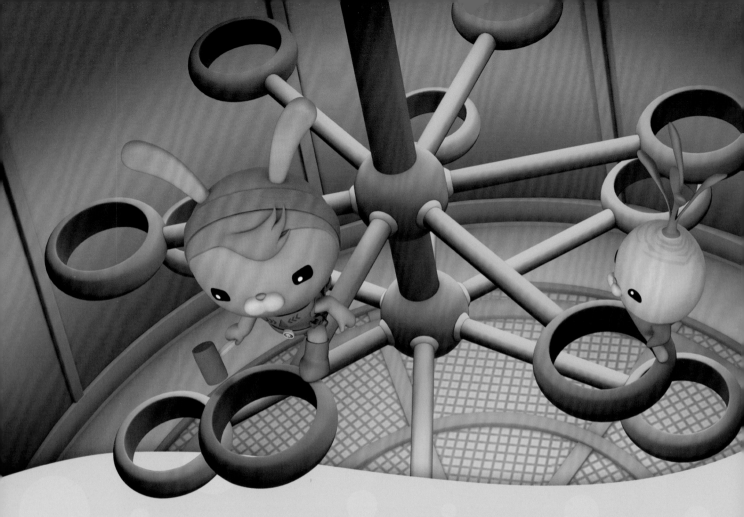

此时，在章鱼堡的引擎舱中，突突兔刚修好了泡泡引擎，接着要给章鱼堡充水。

突突兔按下一个按钮，对小萝卜说："水一旦升到发射台甲板的高度，我们就关上前门。但首先，我们要检查一下章鱼堡的外部是否安全。"

"附近没有生物！"突突兔查看了一下显示屏，转头对小萝卜说。可是，她不知道，就在她转头的那一刻，狮宝靠近了章鱼堡。

紧接着，突突兔按下了吸水按钮，水流涌入章鱼堡中。随后，突突兔激活了头盔。

"现在，我们来测试一下你的尾鳍……"皮医生说完，一回头发现狮宝不见了。他低头一看，发现狮宝快被吸进章鱼堡里了，皮医生连忙追了上去。

"皮医生！"狮宝害怕地叫着。

引擎舱里的突突兔和小萝卜还没发现异样。突然，突突兔被什么东西刺了一下，她低头一看，惊呆了，连忙呼叫巴克队长。

"怎么了，突突兔？"巴克队长立刻回应。

"下面出现了一些状况！"突突兔说道。

dào dǐ shì shén me qíng kuàng
"到底是什么情况？"bā kè duì zhǎng zhuī wèn dào巴克队长追问道。

yīng gāi shuō suàn shì
"应该说算是……chù shǒu lèi shēng wù de yì xiē zhuàngkuàng触手类生物的一些状况！"

tū tū tù yóu yù de huí dá zhe
突突兔犹豫地回答着。

hěn kuài
很快，shī bǎo hé gēn zài hòu miàn de pí yī shēng yì qǐ bèi xī jìn狮宝和跟在后面的皮医生一起被吸进

le zhāng yú bǎo
了章鱼堡。

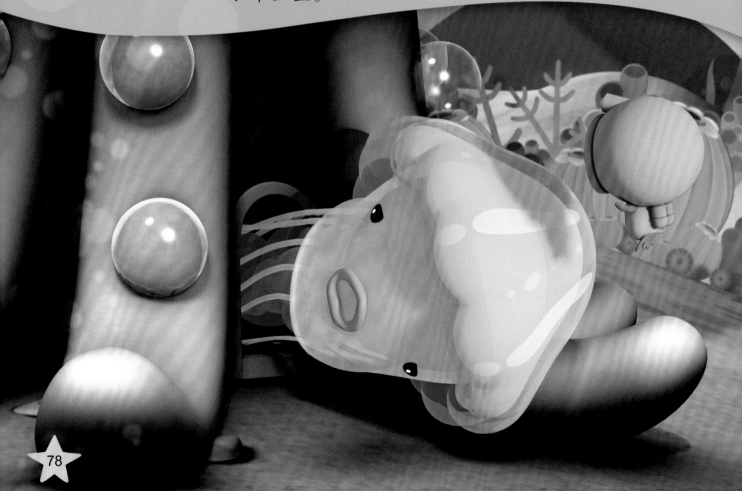

这时，突突兔突然想到了什么，她看了一下显示屏，赶紧汇报：“还有一件事，章鱼堡发大水了。”

基地总部的巴克队长还没来得及搞清楚情况，就被水流冲走了。坐在床上看书的呱唧也没能幸免，水流涌了过来，他还被触手刺了一下。

紧急时刻，突突兔一边费力地游动，一边大喊道："小萝卜！关上……舱门！"小萝卜听了，迅速向上游，对着控制舱门的按钮猛地敲了一锤，舱门立刻关上了。

"这是怎么了？"狮宝感到疑惑不解。

"抱歉，大家伙。我们刚刚好像把你吸进章鱼堡了……"突突兔连忙向狮宝道歉。

皮医生看舱门关闭了，顺手解开了一只触手，安抚着狮宝："但我们会让你，还有你的触手回归大海的。"

　　　　　　　　dàn wǒ de péng you zěn me bàn　　　　　　　shī bǎo hěn dān xīn péng you men de ān wēi　　　pīn mìng xiǎng zhèng
　　　"但我的朋友怎么办？"狮宝很担心朋友们的安危，拼命想挣

tuō shù fù　　　kě shì chù shǒu dōu bèi chán zhù le
脱束缚，可是触手都被缠住了。

　　　　　　shī bǎo　　tíng xià　　zhè yàng nǐ　huì shòu shāng de　　　　pí yī shēng lián máng zhì zhǐ　　　tū tū tù
　　　"狮宝，停下，这样你会受伤的！"皮医生连忙制止。突突兔

hé xiǎo luó bo kàn zhe shī bǎo　　bù zhī gāi zěn me bàn
和小萝卜看着狮宝，不知该怎么办。

zhè shí　　bā kè duì zhǎng yóu le guò lái　　ràng wǒ men lái bāng zhù nǐ hé nǐ de péng you ba

这时，巴克队长游了过来，"让我们来帮助你和你的朋友吧。"

hǎo ba　　shī bǎo yóu yù zhe dā ying le　　dàn shì dòng zuò yào kuài

"好吧！"狮宝犹豫着答应了，"但是动作要快！"

bā kè duì zhǎng ràng xiǎo luó bo liú zài zhè lǐ péi zhe shī bǎo　　rán hòu xià lìng ràng qí tā rén zài jī

巴克队长让小萝卜留在这里陪着狮宝，然后下令让其他人在基

dì zǒng bù jí hé

地总部集合。

很快，海底小纵队就聚集在了基地总部，巴克队长看着眼前纠缠着的触手，向大家解释道："这些是狮鬃水母狮宝的触手。"

突突兔看着显示屏说："你们看，到处都是！"

méi cuò　　 néng yǒu zhè me cháng de chù shǒu　　 fēi shī zōng shuǐ mǔ mò shǔ　　　 xiè líng tōng jī dòng
"没错！能有这么长的触手，非狮鬃水母莫属！"谢灵通激动

de diào chū shī zōng shuǐ mǔ de tú piàn　　 shuō dào　　 shī zōng shuǐ mǔ shì quán shì jiè zuì dà de shuǐ mǔ　 yǒu
地调出狮鬃水母的图片，说道，"狮鬃水母是全世界最大的水母，有

lán jīng nà me cháng　　 ér qiě tā men de chù shǒu tōng cháng néng wèi xiǎo yú tí gōng bǎo hù
蓝鲸那么长，而且他们的触手通常能为小鱼提供保护。"

此时，在章鱼堡外，狗鲨正在追逐失去了保护的船头鱼。

"我可以保护鱼儿们，我的触手没有毒刺，但还是能……哈哈！"

章教授演示了一下，"喷射墨汁的！"

巴克队长同意了，但是让章教授注意安全。章教授走后，巴克队长转头向皮医生请教解绷带的诀窍。

"全靠我的双鳍。"说着，皮医生示范了一遍。

可呱唧没有鳍，他尝试着依靠手腕，但没有成功。

皮医生鼓励道："再试一次，先深呼吸，再发出这样的声音，'哈嚓嘿呀'！"

guā jī zhào zhe pí yī shēng de huà zuò　　kuài sù de jiě kāi le chù shǒu
呱唧照着皮医生的话做，快速地解开了触手，

dá xī xī hé tū tū tù yě dōu chénggōng le
达西西和突突兔也都成功了。

zhāng yú bǎo wài　　zhāng
章鱼堡外，章

jiào shòuzhèng dào chù xún zhǎo nà qún
教授正到处寻找那群

chuán tóu yú
船头鱼。

88

"鱼跑到哪里去了？"章教授正疑惑呢，突然听到了身后的救命声，是船头鱼们。

这时，几只狗鲨游了过来，大叫道："章鱼，别挡路。这是我们的午餐……哈！凉了可就不好吃了！"

"我以一只小飞象章鱼的身份警告你，到别处觅食去吧。"章教授立刻说道。

gǒu shā yě bù gān shì ruò，tiǎo xìn de shuō dào yào shi bù zǒu ne
狗鲨也不甘示弱，挑衅地说道："要是不走呢？"

nà jiù yào xiǎo xīn wǒ de chù shǒu duì nǐ bú kè qi le zhāng jiào shòu lín wēi bú luàn
"那就要小心我的触手对你不客气了！"章教授临危不乱。

gǒu shā cháo xiào de shuō hā nǐ yì zhī zhāng yú yòu bú xiàng shī zōng shuǐ mǔ yí yàng huì zhē
狗鲨嘲笑地说："哈！你一只章鱼，又不像狮鬃水母一样会蜇

rén kuài zǒu kāi
人！快走开。"

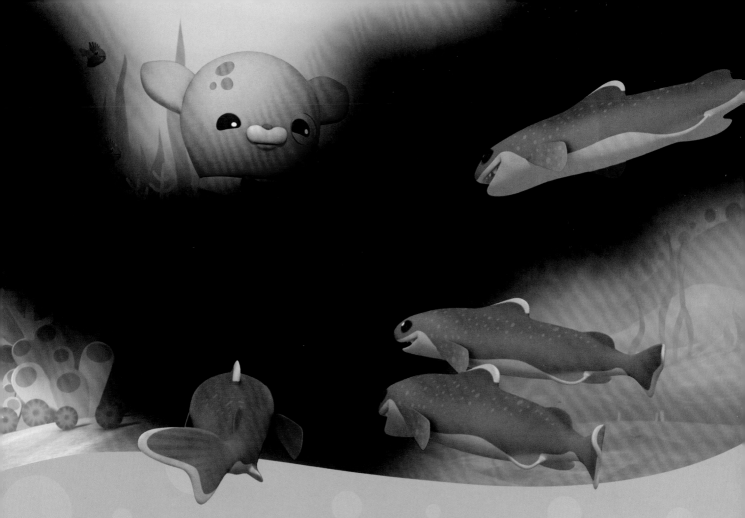

　　　　　nǐ men zì zhǎo de yo　　　　zhāng jiào shòu shuō zhe　　　pēn chū le mò zhī　　　gǒu shā men bèi hēi hēi de
"你们自找的哟！"章教授说着，喷出了墨汁。狗鲨们被黑黑的

mò zhī wéi zhù　　　　shì xiàn wán quán bèi dǎng zhù　le
墨汁围住，视线完全被挡住了。

　　　　　zhāng jiào shòu gǎn jǐn duì chuán tóu yú shuō　　　xiàn zài　　gǎn kuài táo pǎo
　　章教授赶紧对船头鱼说："现在，赶快逃跑！"

　　　　　bù yí huì er　　　mò zhī xiāo sàn le　　　yì zhī gǒu shā kàn le kàn zhōu wéi　　　shuō dào　　　tā men zài
　　不一会儿，墨汁消散了，一只狗鲨看了看周围，说道："他们在

nà er ne　　kuài zhuī
那儿呢！快追！"

在章鱼堡里，基地总部已经被清理完毕，厨房、医务室等各个房间的触手都解开了。很快，发射台的触手也解开了，海底小纵队聚集在发射台，联系上了章教授。

巴克队长问道："章教授，外面怎么样了？"

“队长！我们被狗鲨包围了。我不知道墨汁还能撑多久！我们需要狮宝。”章教授立刻回复道。

“要快！”一只船头鱼补充道。

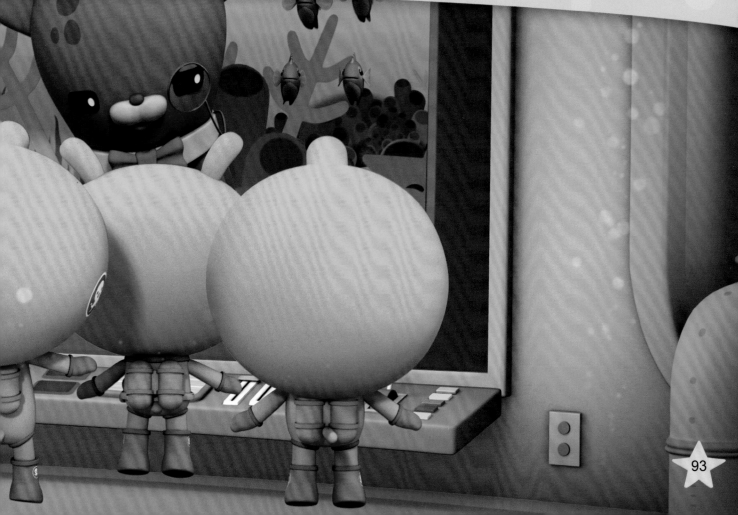

现在只剩下泡泡引擎舱了，可那里的情况太复杂，人越多可能越乱。皮医生决定一个人去，他报告队长后，游向了泡泡引擎舱。

狮宝一见到皮医生，立刻问道："皮医生！怎么了？我什么时候能走啊？"

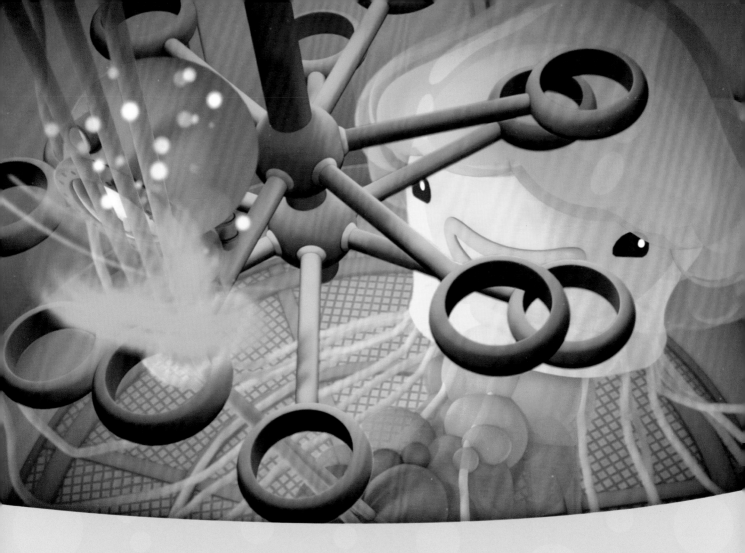

"狮宝，马上就好了，不过可能会有点痒，忍着点。"皮医生平静下来，准备开始工作了。只见皮医生快速地解开了一处又一处打结的触手，引擎舱里时不时地传来狮宝的笑声。

很快，皮医生的任务完成了。

tū tū tù lā xià cāo zòng gǎn　　zhāng yú bǎo cāng mén kāi qǐ le　　shī bǎo gēn suí zhe shuǐ liú
突突兔拉下操纵杆，章鱼堡舱门开启了，狮宝跟随着水流

yóu chū le zhāng yú bǎo
游出了章鱼堡。

shī bǎo yì chū lai jiù tīng jiàn le chuán tóu yú de jiù mìng shēng　　shī bǎo lián máng chōng guo qu
狮宝一出来就听见了船头鱼的救命声。狮宝连忙冲过去，

cháo gǒu shā cì le jǐ xià　　chuán tóu yú men dé jiù le
朝狗鲨刺了几下，船头鱼们得救了。

à　　bù jiū jié de gǎn jué shí zài shì hǎo　　shī bǎo gāo xìng de shuō dào
"啊！不纠结的感觉实在是好！"狮宝高兴地说道。

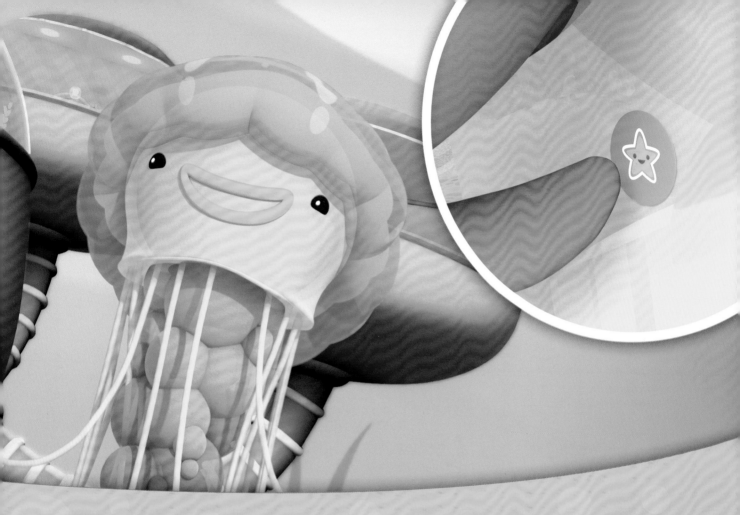

pí yī shēng xiào zhe shuō　　　ér qiě nǐ de chù shǒu kàn qi lai dōu wán hǎo wú sǔn
皮医生笑着说："而且你的触手看起来都完好无损！"

hā hā　　nà xiàn zài jiù kuài gěi wǒ tiē xiào liǎn tiē ba　　shī bǎo shuō　　pí yī shēng
"哈哈！那现在就快给我贴笑脸贴吧！"狮宝说。皮医生

tīng le　　mǎ shàng wèi shī bǎo tiē le gè xiào liǎn tiē
听了，马上为狮宝贴了个笑脸贴。

wǒ yě yào　　wǒ yě yào　　chuán tóu yú men jiāng pí yī shēng tuán tuán wéi zhù　　dà jiā
"我也要，我也要！"船头鱼们将皮医生团团围住。大家

kāi xīn de xiào le
开心地笑了。

 海底报告

欢迎进入本期海底报告，这次我们要介绍的是**狮鬃水母**！

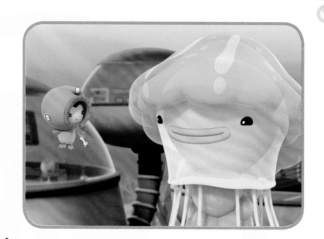

狮鬃水母海里长

海洋世界它最长

它们天生热心肠

保护小鱼身边藏

触手就像长绳子

若是被侵犯，触手蜇敌忙

🐙 装备大揭秘

　　海底小纵队居住在神秘的章鱼堡基地，每当有意外发生，他们就要出发去探险、拯救、保护。行动中，队员们配备了各式各样的装备，这次要介绍的是——防蜇服！

🐙 防蜇服

　　防蜇服也叫深海潜水服，头盔上装有透明面罩、射灯等小部件，它是海底小纵队的常用装备。它可以有效阻挡其他生物的攻击，同时具备较强的抗压功能，非常适合在深海以及危险环境中使用。

雪人蟹

大洋猪

港海豹

海胆入侵

魔鬼鱼

狮子鱼

水熊虫

鸭嘴兽

叶海龙

座头鲸

雪人蟹

海豚传媒官网 http://www.dolphinmedia.cn　海豚微博 http://weibo.com/dolphinmedia

THE ORVILLE

SEASON 1.5 | NEW BEGINNINGS

ORVILLE

SEASON 1.5 | NEW BEGINNINGS

CREATED BY SETH MacFARLANE

SCRIPT
DAVID A. GOODMAN

ART
DAVID CABEZA

COLORS
MICHAEL ATIYEH

LETTERING
RICHARD STARKINGS & COMICRAFT'S JIMMY BETANCOURT

DARK HORSE BOOKS

DESIGNER **BRENNAN THUME**
DIGITAL ART TECHNICIAN **ANN GRAY**

Special thanks to Seth MacFarlane, Andre Bormanis, Brannon Braga, Gerry Duggan, Jason Clark,
Brandon Fayette, Rahne Keith, Joy Fehily, Cassy Brewer, Sheri Conn, and Carol Roeder.

Published by Dark Horse Books
A division of Dark Horse Comics LLC
10956 SE Main Street
Milwaukie, OR 97222

DarkHorse.com

First Edition: February 2020
ISBN 978-1-50671-134-8
Digital ISBN 978-1-50671-138-6

1 3 5 7 9 10 8 6 4 2
Printed in China

This volume collects the Dark Horse comic books *The Orville: New Beginnings Parts 1 & 2* and
The Orville: The Word of Avis Parts 1 & 2.

Library of Congress Cataloging-in-Publication Data
Names: Goodman, David A., 1962- author. | Cabeza, David, 1976- artist. |
    Atiyeh, Michael, colourist. | Starkings, Richard, letterer. |
    Betancourt, Jimmy, letterer.
Title: The Orville season 1.5 : new beginnings / script, David A. Goodman ;
    art, David Cabeza ; colors, Michael Atiyeh ; lettering, Richard
    Starkings & Comicraft's Jimmy Betancourt.
Description: First edition. | Milwaukie, OR : Dark Horse Books, 2020. |
    "This volume collects the Dark Horse comic books The Orville: New
    Beginnings Parts 1 & 2 and The Orville: The Word of Avis Parts 1 & 2" |
    Summary: "Pick up where Seth MacFarlane's TV series leaves off in these
    stories written by The Orville Executive Producer David A. Goodman! In
    "New Beginnings", Ed and Gordon intercept a distress signal from a
    long-lost Union vessel while on their way to a conference. Upon
    investigating, they encounter a new civilization and uncover a piece of
    history that threatens the future of them all. In "The Word of Avis",
    the Orville intervenes when a small transport nearly crosses into Krill
    territory. Its complement of xenoanthropologists blame their own
    carelessness, but when John discovers an old acquaintance among their
    number, the truth is revealed to be far more dangerous"- Provided by
    publisher.
Identifiers: LCCN 2019042007 | ISBN 9781506711348 (paperback)
Subjects: LCSH: Comic books, strips, etc.
Classification: LCC PN6728.O79 G66 2020 | DDC 741.5/973-dc23
LC record available at https://lccn.loc.gov/2019042007

NEW BEGINNINGS PART 1 OF 2

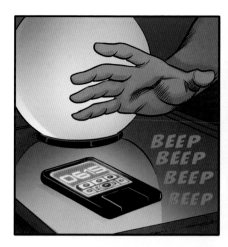

BEEP
BEEP
BEEP
BEEP

I HATE DREAMS.

MAGNETAR DESIGNATED AXP 1E 1048-59, A NEUTRON STAR WITH A VERY POWERFUL MAGNETIC FIELD.

"ISAAC, HOW MUCH LONGER?"

I WOULD ESTIMATE, CAPTAIN, THAT MY INVESTIGATION OF THE MAGNETAR WILL TAKE ANOTHER FORTY-EIGHT POINT NINE SEVEN HOURS--

"YOU KNOW, ED, REALLY EXCITED ABOUT THIS CONFERENCE..."

...FILLING THEM IN ON OUR EXPERIENCE ON THE KRILL SHIP, LOVE PUBLIC SPEAKING.

YOU HATE PUBLIC SPEAKING.

OKAY, YEAH, BUT NOT AS MUCH AS I HATE MAGNETARS.

AND SPEAKING OF "HATE"... UH... WHAT'S GOING ON WITH YOU AND KELLY?

WHAT DO YOU MEAN?

WELL, YOU GOTTA ADMIT, THINGS ARE A LITTLE TENSE ON THE BRIDGE SINCE SHE BROKE UP WITH YOU. *

*WHICH HAPPENED AT THE END OF THE FIRST SEASON EPISODE, "MAD IDOLATRY", A FEW WEEKS BEFORE THIS ADVENTURE.

SHE'S THE ONE WHO'S TENSE. I'M OVER IT.

WHATEVER YOU SAY.

WELL, THAT'S WHAT I'M SAYING. I DON'T HAVE A PROBLEM.

I BELIEVE YOU.

IT WAS A BLOODY CONFLICT, **COST** THOUSANDS OF LIVES... YOU TOOK HISTORY, DIDN'T YOU?

I *TOOK* HISTORY, THAT DOESN'T MEAN I READ ANYTHING.

THE BUOY'S LOG SAYS THE SHIP WAS DAMAGED IN A BATTLE IN A STAR SYSTEM THREE LIGHT YEARS AWAY.

IT'S UNCHARTED.

SHOULD WE GO?

REGULATIONS. DISTRESS CALLS HAVE TO BE ANSWERED, EVEN ONES THAT ARE A HUNDRED YEARS OLD.

RAISE *ORVILLE*, WE SHOULD KEEP THEM APPRISED.

SHUTTLE TO *ORVILLE*, COME IN. SHUTTLE TO *ORVILLE*, DO YOU READ?

THEY'RE NOT READING US. PROBABLY TOO MUCH INTERFERENCE FROM THE MAGNETAR.

STUPID MAGNETAR.

STOP SAYING "MAGNETAR."

LET'S GO.

TO BE BETTER THAN A CONFERENCE."

"YOU JUST SAID YOU WERE LOOKING FORWARD TO GOING."

I LIED.

"EVER SINCE I PUT AN END TO IT, HE'S BEEN REALLY COLD..."

IT'S NO FUN TO WORK HERE ANYMORE.

OH, ARE WE HERE TO HAVE FUN? NOBODY TOLD ME.

YOU KNOW WHAT I MEAN...

LOOK, HE'S HURT, BUT THE LAST THING HE WANTS IS FOR YOU TO LEAVE. THINGS WILL GET EASIER.

PROBABLY WHEN ONE OR BOTH OF YOU FIND OTHER RELATIONSHIPS.

I HOPE HE FINDS HIS FIRST.

OH, SORRY, I WAS JUST LEAVING.

I WOULD APPRECIATE IF YOU WOULD STAY, COMMANDER.

I APOLOGIZE FOR INTERRUPTING. I DID HAVE AN APPOINTMENT.

COME IN. WHAT DID YOU WANT TO SEE ME ABOUT?

I WISH TO ENROLL TOPA IN SCHOOL, BUT THE TEACHER INFORMS ME THAT HE DOES NOT MEET THE AGE REQUIREMENT.

BORTUS, TOPA IS ONLY A FEW MONTHS OLD. THE SCHOOL DOESN'T ACCEPT CHILDREN UNDER THE AGE OF THREE.

HE IS QUITE OLD ENOUGH FOR SCHOOLING. AND KLYDEN HAS BEEN COMPLAINING THAT HE CANNOT SPEND HIS DAY ENTERTAINING HIM.

I'M SORRY, *BUT* THERE'S NOTHING--

WHO THE HELL IS THAT?!

THAT IS TOPA.

I DON'T BELIEVE IT, HE'S ONLY EIGHT MONTHS OLD, BUT HE'S AS DEVELOPED AS A HUMAN BOY OF SEVEN.

THIS WOULD BE NO SURPRISE IF YOU HAD STUDIED MOCLAN CHILD DEVELOPMENT.

DUE TO THE DIFFICULTIES OF SURVIVAL ON MOCLUS, EVOLUTION FAVORED INFANTS WHO MATURED QUICKLY.

HE IS MORE THAN DEVELOPED ENOUGH TO ATTEND YOUR SCHOOL.

I'M NOT ARGUING.

ALL RIGHT. I'LL TALK TO THE TEACHER.

THANK YOU, COMMANDER.

I WISH ED WAS HERE TO SEE THIS...

I WISH KELLY WAS HERE TO SEE THIS...

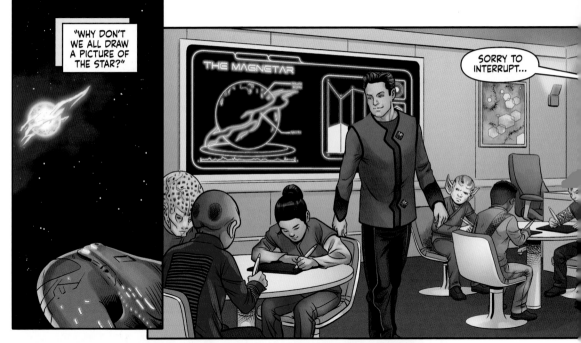

"WHY DON'T WE ALL DRAW A PICTURE OF THE STAR?"

THE MAGNETAR

SORRY TO INTERRUPT...

NO PROBLEM, COMMANDER.

CALL ME KELLY.

WELL, THEN CALL ME CASSIUS.

NICE TO MEET YOU. CAN I HAVE A WORD?

YOU'RE BEING COMPLETELY UNREASONABLE!

I DON'T LIKE PEOPLE TELLING ME MY JOB! HE'S TOO YOUNG!

THE MAGNETAR

HIS DEVELOPMENT IS COMPLETELY DIFFERENT--

NOW YOU'RE GIVING ME A MOCLAN BIOLOGY LESSON?

LOOK--

NO, YOU LOOK!

THESE KIDS ARE MY RESPONSIBILITY, AND PUTTING HIM IN SCHOOL TOO EARLY COULD END UP DOING HIM MORE HARM THAN GOOD.

THE PARENTS FEEL HE'S READY.

PARENTS AREN'T ALWAYS RIGHT!

SOMETIMES THEY JUST WANT THEIR KID OUT OF THE HOUSE AND RATIONALIZE WHY IT'S A GOOD THING.

LOOK, I'M THROUGH ARGUING. INCLUDE TOPA IN THE CLASS.

I'LL FILE A COMPLAINT WITH THE UNION BOARD OF EDUCATION.

THE MAGNETAR

OOOH, BOARD OF EDUCATION, SUPER SCARY.

THE MAGNETAR

OH.

GREETINGS. I AM THOZ.

GREETINGS. I'M... ED, AND THIS IS GORDON.

HELLO.

WE HAVE NOT SEEN YOUR KIND BEFORE. WHAT KIND OF CHOG ARE YOU?

WE'RE NOT "CHOGS." WE'RE CALLED HUMANS.

WELL, WE WELCOME YOU. EVEN THIS LONG AFTER THE CALAMITY, THE PEOPLE OF THE WORLD ARE FINDING THEIR WAY HERE. COME!

GRAYSON TO ISAAC, REPORT PROGRESS.

I WILL BE FINISHED IN EIGHT HOURS, FIFTY SEVEN MINUTES.

VERY WELL, GRAYSON OUT.

HE'S GOING TO WRITE A REALLY LONG REPORT.

I HOPE SOMEONE BESIDES HIM *READS* IT.

BING

COME.

SORRY TO INTERRUPT. COMMANDER, DO YOU HAVE A MINUTE?

A MINUTE.

I'LL STEP OUT.

NO, IT'S OKAY, STAY, IT'LL JUST TAKE A SECOND.

I JUST WANTED TO APOLOGIZE. YOU WERE RIGHT.

REALLY?

YEAH, TOPA DID FINE IN HIS FIRST CLASS. I GUESS I COULD'VE USED A LECTURE ON MOCLAN BIOLOGY.

SO... NO COMPLAINTS TO THE BOARD OF EDUCATION?

NO COMPLAINTS. I'LL LET YOU GET BACK TO WORK.

HE'S CUTE.

YOU SHOULD ASK HIM OUT.

I WAS THINKING HE'S MORE YOUR TYPE.

NO THANKS. I'D BE CRAZY TO DATE SOMEONE ABOARD THIS SHIP.

REALLY?

THAT'S NOT VERY REALISTIC.

WHY NOT?

WELL, YOU'RE PROBABLY GOING TO BE ON THIS SHIP FOR A FEW YEARS, RIGHT?

IF ALL GOES WELL.

SO... YOUR PLAN IS TO STAY CELIBATE THAT WHOLE TIME?

NEW BEGINNINGS PART 2 OF 2

THEY MUST HAVE USED IT TO FIRE THE CANNON.

THE PENGUINS SHOT US DOWN?

I DON'T KNOW, THEY'RE SO PRIMITIVE. WE'VE GOT TO FIND OUT MORE...

I'VE NEVER BEEN ON ONE OF THESE OLD BATTLESHIPS.

REALLY? THERE'S ONE IN THE FLEET MUSEUM.

YEAH, NOT REALLY A "MUSEUM" GUY...

YOU WERE SAYING THEY WERE TOO PRIMITIVE...?

I DON'T BELIEVE IT.

THEY'VE TURNED THIS WHOLE SHIP INTO A GLORIFIED DRIVE-THRU.

BIG MAC, LARGE FRIES, DIET COKE.

YOU CAN CHOOSE TO EAT ANYTHING IN THE WORLD, AND YOU CHOOSE... MUD?

MAYBE THEY CAN'T CHOOSE ANYTHING... EVERYTHING'S ON A LOW POWER LEVEL.

IF IT'S PRESET, IT DOESN'T REQUIRE ANY USE OF THE COMPUTER.

MAYBE WE CAN SNOOP AROUND A LITTLE. COME ON.

MY FRIENDS, YOU CAN'T GO IN THERE, IT'S FORBIDDEN.

COME, JOIN US TO EAT AND SING IN PRAISE.

OH, SORRY...

WHY IS IT FORBIDDEN, THOZ?

IT JUST IS AND ALWAYS HAS BEEN. COME.

THINK THOZ KNEW WHAT WE WERE UP TO--?

I DON'T KNOW. WE HAVE TO FIND OUT MORE, BEFORE THE *ORVILLE* COMES LOOKING FOR US.

I HOPE IT'S SOON. THIS FOOD IS TERRIBLE.

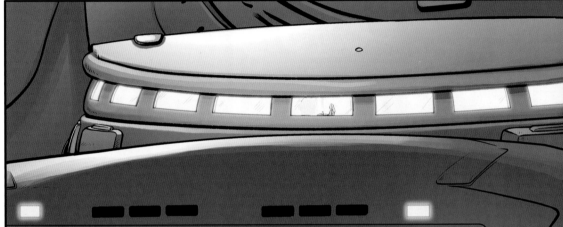

BEAUTIFUL, ISN'T IT?

IT IS...

YOU'RE UP LATE...

I LIKE THE QUIET. MIND IF I JOIN YOU?

LOOK, CASSIUS, YOU'RE A NICE GUY, BUT MY LIFE IS REALLY COMPLICATED. IN CASE YOU DIDN'T KNOW, MY COMMANDING OFFICER IS ALSO MY EX-HUSBAND, BUT OF COURSE YOU KNEW THAT, EVERYBODY KNOWS THAT, SO YOU CAN UNDERSTAND I HAVE TO TREAD REALLY CAREFULLY, AND SOMETIMES I HAVE TO PUT MY PERSONAL LIFE ON HOLD...

...THAT'S NOT TO SAY I'M NOT INTERESTED, I AM, YOU'RE SUCH A NICE GUY... I KNOW, I SAID THAT ALREADY, BUT I REALLY MEAN IT, AND IF THINGS WERE DIFFERENT I WOULD LOVE TO SEE WHERE THIS TAKES US...

...BUT I JUST DON'T THINK IT'D BE GOOD FOR EITHER ONE OF US. I HOPE YOU UNDERSTAND.

UH... OKAY, SINCE OUR RELATIONSHIP IS ALREADY A HUGE DISASTER, THERE'S NO HARM IN ME SITTING HERE AND LOOKING AT THE STAR WITH YOU, RIGHT?

YEAH, SURE...

COMMANDER, I HAVE FINISHED MY STUDY OF THE MAGNETAR.

A FEW HOURS EARLY.

I AM VERY EFFICIENT.

OR DID YOU SET A GOAL THAT YOU KNEW YOU'D BEAT?

NEGATIVE, LIEUTENANT. MY INITIAL ESTIMATE WAS BASED ON THE LIMITATIONS OF UNION EQUIPMENT WHICH I COMPENSATED FOR BY SIMULTANEOUSLY UPGRADING THE SCANNER ARRAY.

VERY EFFICIENT. HELM, TAKE US OUT OF ORBIT AND SET COURSE FOR OUTPOST 23.

HEY, BORTUS, HOW'S TOPA LIKING SCHOOL?

HE ENJOYS IT, BUT KLYDEN IS DISATISFIED.

WHAT'S THE PROBLEM NOW?

THE TEACHER DOES NOT INCLUDE COMBAT TRAINING IN THE CURRICULUM.

GUESS YOU'LL HAVE TO GET HIM A TUTOR.

THAT IS OUR INTENTION.

COMMANDER, WE'VE CLEARED THE INTERFERENCE AND ARE RECEIVING A MESSAGE FROM OUTPOST 23...

...THE CAPTAIN AND GORDON NEVER ARRIVED.

NO SIGN OF THEM? NO DISTRESS CALL?

NO, SIR.

PREPARE TO CONDUCT A SEARCH. WE'RE GOING TO RETRACE THEIR STEPS.

HELM, TAKE US TO QUANTUM. MATCH THE SHUTTLE'S COURSE EXACTLY.

NO POWER HERE AT ALL.

I'M GOING TO TRY TO TRANSFER SOME OF MY COMSCANNER'S TO THIS PANEL.

THERE'S A MESSAGE...

HOW'D YOU KNOW THIS IS WHERE THE MESSAGE WOULD BE?

IT'S WHERE I WOULD PUT IT.

I'M ENSIGN HODGES... RELIEF NAVIGATOR... OUR TASK FORCE WAS SUCKERED INTO THIS UNCHARTED SYSTEM WITH A FALSE DISTRESS SIGNAL.

THE BATTLE'S OVER... BURTON'S THE ONLY SHIP LEFT, SO WE WON, I GUESS, AND WE CRASHED ON THE PLANET...

...ALL THE SENIOR OFFICERS KILLED... I'M THE MOST SENIOR... I'M IN COMMAND.

OUR CRASH... KILLED THE PLANET..

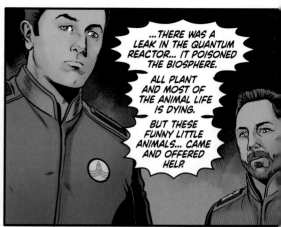

...THERE WAS A LEAK IN THE QUANTUM REACTOR... IT POISONED THE BIOSPHERE.

ALL PLANT AND MOST OF THE ANIMAL LIFE IS DYING.

BUT THESE FUNNY LITTLE ANIMALS... CAME AND OFFERED HELP.

THEY WANT TO HELP US. THEY DON'T KNOW THEY'RE GOING TO DIE BECAUSE OF WHAT WE DID.

ME AND THE CREW, THERE'S ABOUT TWENTY OF US, ARE NOT GOING TO LET THAT HAPPEN. I DON'T KNOW WHAT WE CAN DO, BUT WE'RE GOING TO DO SOMETHING.

WE'VE GOT TO DO SOMETHING, THEY DIDN'T ASK TO BE A PART OF THIS.

HODGES OUT.

THEY REPAIRED THE REACTOR AND HOOKED IT UP TO THE FOOD SYNTHESIZER, MADE THAT PARTICLE CANNON TO PROTECT THE CHOGS...

...AND IT'S ALL FUNCTIONED FOR A HUNDRED YEARS. KID DID GOOD WORK.

WE CAN'T BE THE REASON IT ALL FALLS APART. COME ON.

WHAT DO YOU MEAN?

ORVILLE IS GOING TO FIND THE SAME TRAIL OF BREADCRUMBS THAT LED US HERE. WHICH MEANS IT'LL BE A TARGET FOR THE PARTICLE CANNON.

YEAH, BUT THE ORVILLE CAN TAKE A PUNCH BETTER THAN THE SHUTTLE.

THAT'S NOT WHAT I'M WORRIED ABOUT.

IF ORVILLE FIRES BACK, ONE SHOT COULD BE ENOUGH TO BLOW THE REACTOR, AND KILL EVERYONE AND EVERYTHING IN A ONE KILOMETER RADIUS.

OH, YEAH, THAT WOULDN'T BE GOOD.

HODGES AND HIS CREW DID THEIR BEST TO PROTECT THE CHOGS. WE OWE IT TO ALL OF THEM TO TRY TO DO THE SAME.

I'M GOING TO SET MY COMSCANNER TO SEND OUT A REGULAR MESSAGE TO *ORVILLE* TO RAISE THEIR DEFLECTOR SCREENS AND HOLD THEIR FIRE. THAT'LL BUY US A LITTLE TIME ONCE THEY'RE IN ORBIT.

ED...

NO ONE IS ALLOWED IN THE FOOD PLACE.

THOZ, I CAN EXPLAIN...

TAKE THEM!

OW! GUYS, TAKE IT EASY... WE'RE ALL PALS...

THOZ, PLEASE, WE CAN HELP-- *AHHH!*

ISAAC, ANYTHING?

THE DISTRESS SIGNAL LT. KITAN RECEIVED IS COMING FROM THIS GENERAL VICINITY.

AS FAINT AS IT IS, IS IT LIKELY THAT ED AND GORDON PICKED IT UP?

IT WOULD SEEM PROBABLE.

I AM DETECTING AN OBJECT, THIRTY-TWO DEGREES TO STARBOARD.

LET'S SEE IT.

ON SCREEN.

UNION SHIP COMMUNICATIONS BUOY. AN OLD ONE.

IT BELONGS TO THE BCV *BURTON*, A UNION VESSEL LOST IN THE WAR WITH THE TZEL.

THAT WAS LIKE A HUNDRED YEARS AGO.

ISAAC, SEE IF YOU CAN INTERFACE WITH THE BUOY.

AYE, SIR.

WHAT DO YOU HOPE TO FIND?

I DON'T KNOW. BUT IT'S WHAT ED WOULD'VE DONE.

"ED?"

"ED? YOU OKAY..."

OH BOY...

HOW LONG HAVE I BEEN OUT?

I DON'T KNOW, THEY TOOK OUR COMSCANNERS AND I'M NOT WEARING A WATCH.

DID YOU GET A CHANCE TO SET THAT SIGNAL?

NO...

WHAT WERE YOU DOING IN THE FOOD PLACE?

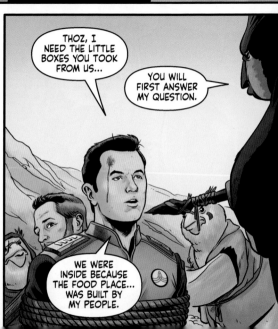

THOZ, I NEED THE LITTLE BOXES YOU TOOK FROM US...

YOU WILL FIRST ANSWER MY QUESTION.

WE WERE INSIDE BECAUSE THE FOOD PLACE... WAS BUILT BY MY PEOPLE.

WHAT DO YOU MEAN, "YOUR PEOPLE?"

WE COME FROM SOMEPLACE ELSE. THOZ, DO YOU KNOW THAT AT ONE TIME THIS WORLD WAS VERY DIFFERENT?

I HAVE HEARD MANY STORIES, YES.

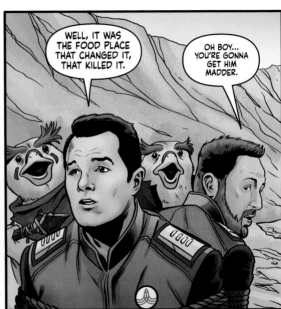

WELL, IT WAS THE FOOD PLACE THAT CHANGED IT, THAT KILLED IT.

OH BOY... YOU'RE GONNA GET HIM MADDER.

HOW COULD IT DO THAT?

THE FOOD PLACE IS A SHIP... OR WAS A SHIP... THAT FLIES. WHEN IT CRASHED, IT LEAKED A POISON THAT KILLED THE LIFE ON YOUR PLANET.

I'M NOT WITH HIM. WE BARELY KNOW EACH OTHER.

WHAT YOU SAY IS RIDICULOUS. THE FOOD PLACE IS A BUILDING. IT PROTECTS US AND FEEDS US.

YES, BUT... WAIT, THOZ, YOU SAID YOU'VE HEARD STORIES ABOUT THE WORLD AS IT WAS. FROM WHO?

FROM THE ELDERS WHO LIVED DURING THAT TIME.

ARE ANY OF THEM STILL ALIVE?

THERE IS ONE.

TAKE US TO HIM. HE MIGHT HELP ME PROVE WHAT I'M SAYING. ALL OUR LIVES DEPEND ON IT.

VERY WELL.

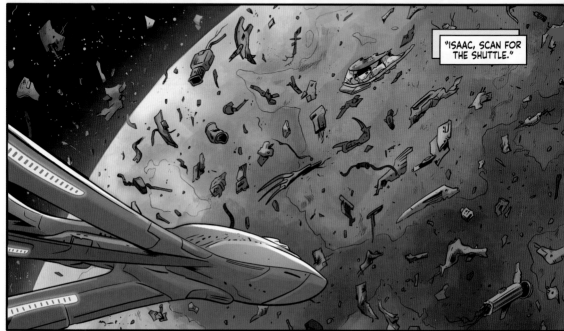

"ISAAC, SCAN FOR THE SHUTTLE."

I CANNOT SCAN THE PLANET'S SURFACE THROUGH THE DEBRIS FIELD, HOWEVER I AM PICKING UP AN ION TRAIL THAT COULD HAVE BEEN PRODUCED BY THE SHUTTLE'S ENGINES.

ALARA...

I'VE HAILED THEM, NO RESPONSE.

WE'LL NEED TO SCAN THE PLANET. HELM, TAKE US INTO A LOW ORBIT.

I AM ROP. I AM ONE HUNDRED AND SEVEN YEARS OLD.

I JUST WANT TO SAY YOU LOOK GREAT. DO YOU EAT YOGURT, IS THAT YOUR THING?

WHAT IS IT YOU WANT OF ME?

ROP, DO YOU REMEMBER WHEN YOU CAME TO LIVE HERE? WHEN THE WORLD STARTED TO CHANGE?

YES. I WAS VERY YOUNG. MUCH OF MY FAMILY DIED THEN.

DO YOU REMEMBER MEN LIKE ME WHO LIVED IN THE FOOD PLACE?

YES... IT HAS BEEN SO LONG I'D FORGOTTEN THEM... BUT YES...

ONE NAMED HODGES.

HODGES. HE WANTED TO HELP US. HE BROUGHT US ALL HERE.

HMMMMMMMMM

WHAT'S THAT SOUND--

OH NO...

HMMMM CHGUNG

"ED, THEY'RE HERE."

WHO THE HELL'S FIRING AT US?

IT IS A SHIP ON THE SURFACE. IT IS THE BURTON.

THAT HUNDRED YEAR-OLD SHIP PACKS A WALLOP... TARGET THEM...

HOW CAN YOU KNOW OF HODGES?

HE WAS OF MY PEOPLE. AND I'M LIKE HIM, I WANT TO HELP YOU.

YOU REMEMBER THE GRASS AND THE TREES OF YOUR WORLD? AND THE WATER, ALL THE WATER THAT USED TO BE ON THE GROUND?

YES, AS OLD AS I AM, I HAVE NOT FORGOTTEN.

MY PEOPLE CAN BRING THAT ALL BACK. WE BUILT THE FOOD PLACE, BUT WE CAN DO MUCH MORE NOW. YOU JUST HAVE TO TRUST ME AND GIVE ME THE BOXES THAT YOU TOOK FROM ME.

DO YOU BELIEVE HIM?

I DON'T KNOW. BUT IF THERE IS A CHANCE...

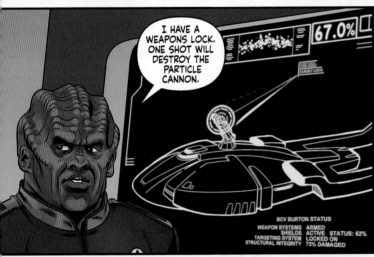

I HAVE A WEAPONS LOCK. ONE SHOT WILL DESTROY THE PARTICLE CANNON.

67.0%

BCV BURTON STATUS
WEAPON SYSTEMS — ARMED
SHIELDS — ACTIVE STATUS: 52%
TARGETING SYSTEM — LOCKED ON
STRUCTURAL INTEGRITY — 73% DAMAGED

RETURN FIRE...

KELLY, IT'S ED! WHATEVER YOU DO, DON'T FIRE!

BORTUS!

I DID NOT FIRE.

WHEW. ED, ARE YOU OKAY?

LONG STORY, JUST GET TO A HIGH ORBIT.

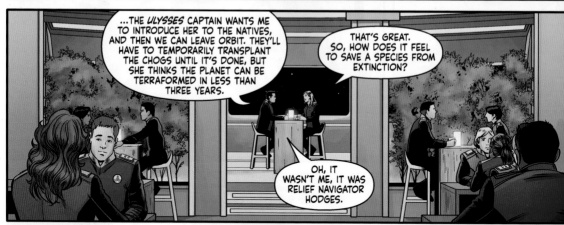

...THE *ULYSSES* CAPTAIN WANTS ME TO INTRODUCE HER TO THE NATIVES, AND THEN WE CAN LEAVE ORBIT. THEY'LL HAVE TO TEMPORARILY TRANSPLANT THE CHOGS UNTIL IT'S DONE, BUT SHE THINKS THE PLANET CAN BE TERRAFORMED IN LESS THAN THREE YEARS.

THAT'S GREAT. SO, HOW DOES IT FEEL TO SAVE A SPECIES FROM EXTINCTION?

OH, IT WASN'T ME, IT WAS RELIEF NAVIGATOR HODGES.

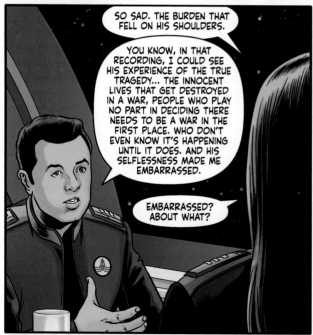

SO SAD. THE BURDEN THAT FELL ON HIS SHOULDERS.

YOU KNOW, IN THAT RECORDING, I COULD SEE HIS EXPERIENCE OF THE TRUE TRAGEDY... THE INNOCENT LIVES THAT GET DESTROYED IN A WAR, PEOPLE WHO PLAY NO PART IN DECIDING THERE NEEDS TO BE A WAR IN THE FIRST PLACE. WHO DON'T EVEN KNOW IT'S HAPPENING UNTIL IT DOES. AND HIS SELFLESSNESS MADE ME EMBARRASSED.

EMBARRASSED? ABOUT WHAT?

ABOUT WHAT A DICK I'VE BEEN LATELY. TO YOU.

CAPTAIN'S PREROGATIVE.

WELL, I'M SORRY.

THANKS.

SO, ANYTHING HAPPEN WHILE I WAS AWAY I NEED TO KNOW ABOUT?

NOTHING THAT CAN'T WAIT.

THE WORD OF AVIS PART 1 OF 2

"UNIDENTIFIED SHIP, THIS IS CAPTAIN ED MERCER OF THE U.S.S. ORVILLE..."

...YOU'RE ABOUT TO CROSS INTO KRILL TERRITORY... REVERSE COURSE IMMEDIATELY.

NO RESPONSE, SIR.

GORDON, CLOSE THE DISTANCE.

BORTUS, LOCK ON TRACTOR BEAM...

WE SNAGGED 'EM.

TRACTOR LOCKED ON...

LET'S GET AS FAR AWAY FROM KRILL TERRITORY AS WE CAN. GORDON, BRING US ABOUT--

CAPTAIN, THEY HAVE NOT POWERED DOWN THEIR ENGINES.

WHAT?

ALARA, HAIL THEM AGAIN.

UNIDENTIFIED SHIP, CUT YOUR ENGINES...

NO RESPONSE, SIR...

WHAT ARE THEY DOING? THEIR ENGINES AREN'T POWERFUL ENOUGH TO BREAK AWAY.

THEIR ENGINES ARE OVERHEATING.

THEY'RE GOING TO BLOW THEMSELVES UP!

LAMARR TO BRIDGE, I GOT AN IDEA...

...I THINK I CAN LINK TO THEIR ENGINEERING PANEL AND SHUT DOWN THEIR ENGINES FROM HERE.

DO IT!

DANN, HOOK US UP...

"...WE DON'T GOT A LOT OF TIME..."

UNION TRANSPORT VESSEL

THEIR ENGINES WILL OVERLOAD...

...IN FOUR POINT SEVEN SECONDS.

IF WE CUT THE TRACTOR BEAM, IT'LL BE LIKE SNAPPING A RUBBER BAND, AND THEY'LL FLY OFF INTO KRILL SPACE.

BRIDGE TO LAMARR, STATUS!

YOU'RE CONNECTED TO THEIR CONTROL PANEL... BUT THERE'S SOME WEIRD FEEDBACK...

IGNORE IT... SCRAMMING THEIR REACTOR...

"ENGINES SHUTDOWN."

GOOD JOB, JOHN. BORTUS, TRACTOR THEM INTO THE BAY.

THAT'S A SHIP FULL OF ASSHOLES...

I CONCUR WITH LIEUTENANT MALLOY.

ALL RIGHT, WE DON'T KNOW WHO WE'RE DEALING WITH INSIDE, BUT GIVEN HOW THEY TRIED TO RUN, THEY COULD BE DANGEROUS.

WE ARE READY...

I'M VERY SORRY...

...MY NAME'S DARDEN, AND THERE'S BEEN A TERRIBLE MISUNDERSTANDING.

...I'M A XENOANTHROPOLOGIST, AND I'M AFRAID I'VE NEGLECTED THE REGULAR MAINTENANCE OF MY SHIP.

OUR SENSORS AND COMMUNICATIONS WERE OUT, WE THOUGHT YOU WERE SOME KIND OF PIRATES...

YOU WERE HEADED DIRECTLY INTO KRILL SPACE...

ALSO MY FAULT, THE NAVIGATIONAL COMPUTER IS PROVING DIFFICULT.

WE'RE JUST A GROUP OF ACADEMICS HEADING TO STUDY THE PRIMITIVE CULTURE ON MIZAR II.

WELL, I'M GOING TO HAVE TO REPORT THIS TO UNION CENTRAL.

IN THE MEANTIME, YOU'LL BE OUR GUESTS. LT. KITAN WILL SHOW YOU AND YOUR COMPANIONS TO QUARTERS.

THAT'S VERY GRACIOUS OF YOU. THANK YOU.

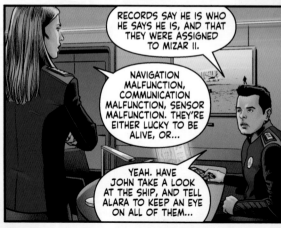

RECORDS SAY HE IS WHO HE SAYS HE IS, AND THAT THEY WERE ASSIGNED TO MIZAR II.

NAVIGATION MALFUNCTION, COMMUNICATION MALFUNCTION, SENSOR MALFUNCTION. THEY'RE EITHER LUCKY TO BE ALIVE, OR...

YEAH. HAVE JOHN TAKE A LOOK AT THE SHIP, AND TELL ALARA TO KEEP AN EYE ON ALL OF THEM...

UNION POINT GRADUATION.

SO WHERE YOU FROM, CELESTE...

I'M YAPHIT, BY THE WAY...

I DIDN'T KNOW YOU WERE ON THE ORVILLE.

YEAH, CHIEF ENGINEER. I REMEMBER YOU HAVE SOME SKILLS IN THAT TOO.

OH, I LEFT IT BEHIND. I'M A XENOANTHROPOLOGIST.

WHICH IS HOW WE GOT IN THIS MESS.

WELL, WE CAN HELP YOU OUT.

JOHN LAMARR, COMING TO MY RESCUE.

YOU LIKE THE BEACH, CELESTE?

GIVE IT UP, DANN, WE'RE DONE.

MAY WE JOIN YOU, LIEUTENANT MALLOY?

UH... SURE...

IT SOUNDS THRILLING. TELL US MORE.

"THESE GUYS ARE NOT ASSHOLES..."

...THEY'RE NUTJOBS. THEY WERE ACTUALLY JEALOUS OF ME GETTING TO GO TO KRILL CHURCH.

I'M MORE CONCERNED THE TEAM TASKED WITH EXAMINING THE ANKHANA ALSO JUST HAPPENED TO GET LOST NEAR KRILL SPACE.

IT WOULD SEEM AN UNLIKELY COINCIDENCE.

JOHN, ANYTHING SUSPICIOUS ABOUT THEIR SHIP?

WELL, THEIR SYSTEMS WERE DEFINITELY DAMAGED. BUT THEIR ENGINEER...

WHAT ABOUT HER?

I WAS AT UNION POINT WITH HER. SHE WAS VERY COMPETENT IN ENGINEERING.

IT DOESN'T SEEM POSSIBLE THAT SHE'D LET ALL THOSE SYSTEMS FAIL.

COULD THEY BE... KRILL SPIES?

I'VE EXAMINED THEM. THEY ARE WHO THEY SAY THE ARE...

...ALTHOUGH I SUPPOSE THE KRILL MIGHT HAVE SOME TECHNOLOGY THAT WOULD ALLOW THEM TO DISGUISE THEMSELVES.

SO... BASICALLY WE'VE GOT NOTHING.

WE'LL JUST HAVE TO KEEP A CLOSE EYE ON THEM.

HEY...

JOHN, HEY.

I WAS JUST COMING BY TO SEE IF I COULD BUY YOU A DRINK.

I WISH I COULD, I HAVE TO GET TO A MEETING.

A MEETING?

YES, WE'RE GOING TO BE GETTING UNDERWAY SOON AND DR. DARDEN WANTS TO GO OVER SAFETY PROTOCOLS FOR WHEN WE ARRIVE ON MIZAR II.

CAN I GET A RAINCHECK?

DEFINITELY.

WHAT ARE YOU DOING HERE?

CAPTAIN TOLD ME TO KEEP AN EYE ON DARDEN AND HIS TEAM.

NOW THEY'RE ALL IN THERE. DOING WHAT, I DON'T KNOW.

I MAY BE ABLE TO HELP WITH THAT.

I GOT ACCESS TO THEIR SHIP'S CONTROLS. SHOULDN'T BE A PROBLEM TO ACCESS THEIR INTERNAL CAMERAS.

UH... I'D NEED A SECURITY REASON TO AUTHORIZE THAT.

OH. DID YOU HEAR THAT SCREAM? I THINK SOMEONE IN THAT SHIP JUST SCREAMED.

OH. BETTER CHECK THAT OUT.

HERE WE GO. LOOKS LIKE THEY'RE ALL IN THE CARGO BAY.

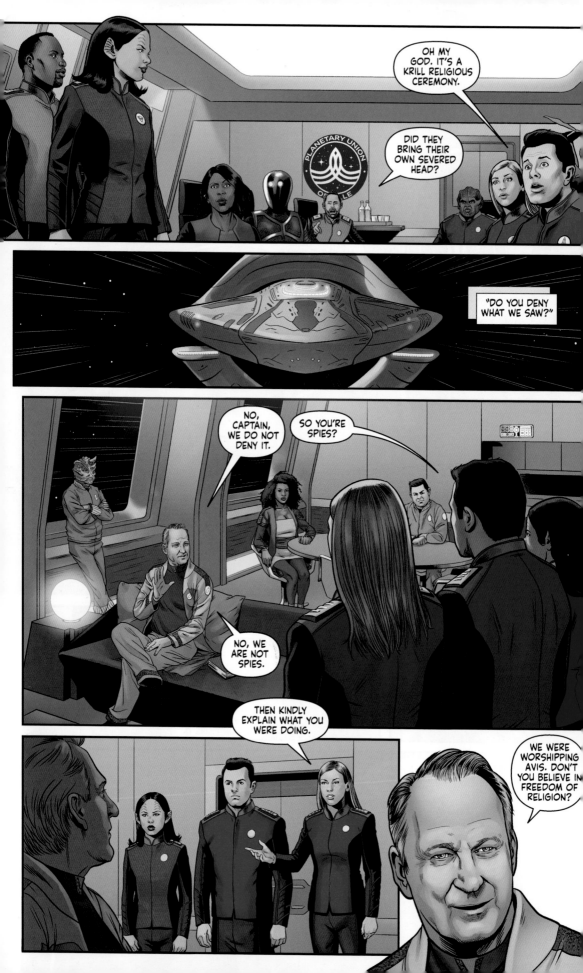

YOU... BELIEVE IN THE KRILL RELIGION?

YES, AND WE HAVE YOUR CAPTAIN TO THANK FOR IT...

"...FOR BRINGING ME THE ANKHANA. ADMIRAL HALSEY ASSIGNED ME AND MY TEAM THE TASK OF STUDYING IT."

WE QUICKLY LEARNED HOW IMPORTANT SCHOLARSHIP IS TO THE KRILL. STUDYING THE ANKHANA IS THE BASIS OF EVERYTHING TO THEM.

"THEN, TO BETTER UNDERSTAND WHO THE KRILL WERE, WE DECIDED TO FOLLOW THE TEACHINGS.

"DAILY STUDY OF THE SCRIPTURE, PRAYER BEFORE MEALS, THE ROLES OF MEN AND WOMEN... WE BEGAN TO FULLY UNDERSTAND THE BELIEF SYSTEM."

BUT GORDON AND I WEREN'T ABLE TO COPY THE ENTIRE ANKHANA.

YES, THERE WERE HOLES IN OUR KNOWLEDGE. SO WE SOUGHT HELP.

TELEYA.

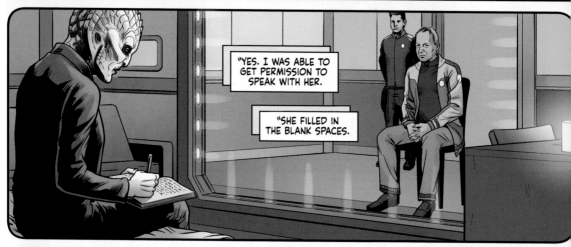

"YES. I WAS ABLE TO GET PERMISSION TO SPEAK WITH HER.

"SHE FILLED IN THE BLANK SPACES.

"SHE EVENTUALLY LED US IN RELIGIOUS TEACHING, AND WE CAME TO UNDERSTAND THE LIFE AVIS OFFERED. STRUCTURE, SECURITY..."

...PURPOSE. WE KNEW WE JUST JOIN OUR PEOPLE.

BUT THAT'S INSANE. THE KRILL WILL KILL YOU ON SIGHT.

YOU'RE WRONG. THEY WILL ACCEPT US.

LOOK, WE RESPECT ALL BELIEFS--

NO YOU DON'T.

KARX IS RIGHT.

YOU LOOK DOWN ON US FOR BELIEVING IN SOMETHING GREATER THAN OURSELVES, SOMETHING THAT GIVES US STRENGTH AND PURPOSE AND A SHARED IDENTITY.

MAYBE I DO. BECAUSE I CAN'T SEE RELIGION AS ANYTHING BUT SUPERSTITION.

WE SHOULD BE ABLE TO DECIDE OUR OWN FATE.

NOT IN THIS CASE. UNDER THE LAWS OF THE PLANETARY UNION, YOU HAVE TO RESPECT THE BORDERS.

AND EVEN IF YOU WON'T, WE HAVE TO PROTECT YOUR LIVES.

YOU MAY NOT HAVE A CHOICE IN THE MATTER, CAPTAIN.

WHAT DO YOU MEAN--

MALLOY TO MERCER. ED, YOU BETTER GET UP HERE.

...WE GOT SOME UNUSUAL FEEDBACK. I THINK THEY MAY HAVE SNUCK THE PROGRAM IN THERE.

I DETECTED THE FEEDBACK. CAPTAIN SHOULD PROBABLY KNOW THAT.

I FOUND THE PROGRAM. IT MUST HAVE BEEN CELESTE WHO SNUCK INTO OUR CONTROL COMPUTER...

...IT'S BEEN SLOWLY PUTTING US ON A DIFFERENT COURSE.

SO THE QUESTION IS, WHERE ARE WE?

I HAVE DETERMINED OUR COORDINATES.

I DON'T THINK I WANT TO KNOW.

I THINK YOU ALREADY DO.

WE ARE IN KRILL TERRITORY...

"...APPROXIMATELY THIRTY-FIVE LIGHT YEARS ACROSS THEIR BORDER."

TO BE CONTINUED...

THIRTY LIGHT YEARS INSIDE KRILL TERRITORY.

GORDON...

WE'RE GOING, WE'RE GOING...

"ED, EVEN AT MAXIMUM SPEED..."

...IT'LL TAKE THREE HOURS TO GET BACK TO UNION SPACE.

IT WILL NOT TAKE THAT LONG, LIEUTENANT. BASED ON MY CALCULATIONS IT WILL TAKE TWO POINT SEVEN EIGHT HOURS.

OH, I FEEL SO MUCH BETTER.

WE'VE BEEN INCREDIBLY LUCKY THE KRILL HAVEN'T DETECTED US ALREADY.

IT IS UNLIKELY THAT "LUCK" WILL CONTINUE.

CAPTAIN, I HAVE AN IDEA...

WHEN WE RESCUED YOU AND COMMANDER GRAYSON FROM THE CALIVON ZOO, ISAAC WAS ABLE TO DISGUISE *ORVILLE* AS A CALIVON SHIP, USING THEIR HOLOGRAPHIC TECHNOLOGY.

WE COULD DO IT AGAIN, ONLY THIS TIME MAKE US LOOK LIKE A KRILL SHIP.

ISAAC?

I AM MAKING THE NECESSARY ADJUSTMENTS...

THEY ARE CONDUCTING A LONG RANGE SCAN.

THE CALIVON SCANNED US TOO, AND THEY LET US PASS.

IT IS WHAT IT APPEARS TO BE.

THEN WHY, SAZERON, IS SOMETHING IN MY HEAD TELLING ME IT ISN'T?

THE ANKHANA TEACHES "DO NOT TURN A DEAF EAR TO THE WHISPER, FOR THAT IS THE VOICE OF AVIS."

SCAN IT WITH NEUTRON RADIATION.

NEUTRON RADIATION? WHAT WILL THAT SHOW?

I DO NOT KNOW FOR SURE. BUT AS THE SAZERON ADVISED, I AM LISTENING TO THE WHISPER.

VERY WELL.

CAPTAIN, THEY'RE SCANNING US.

AGAIN?

THIS SCANNING BEAM IS DIFFERENT. IT CONTAINS NEUTRON RADIATION.

ED, ISN'T THAT WHAT SCREWED UP OUR HOLOGRAPHIC DISGUISES?

OH CRAP.

THE HOLOGRAPHIC GENERATOR IS MALFUNCTIONING...

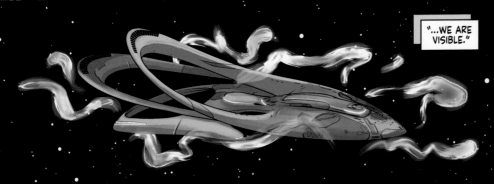

"...WE ARE VISIBLE."

THAT CALIVON THING IS WORTHLESS!

THE HEAVY METALS IN THE ASTEROID ARE INTERFERING WITH THEIR TARGETING SENSORS.

NOW WE JUST HAVE TO HOPE THEY DON'T LAUNCH MISSILES.

THEY HAVE JUST LAUNCHED MISSILES.

MAYBE NEXT TIME KEEP IT TO YOURSELF.

THE MISSILES HAVE SOPHISTICATED GUIDANCE SYSTEMS. THEY HAVE LOCKED ON TO US.

WE'LL NEED COVER.

GORDON, GET US CLOSER TO THAT BIG ONE.

CLOSER?

IT'S
GOING TO BE
CLOSE.

WE'RE IN!

ED, THE OPENING...

"...WE'RE SEALED IN."

IT WOULD APPEAR THAT THE MISSILES' DETONATIONS RESULTED IN A CAVE IN.

WELL, THAT'LL MAKE IT HARDER FOR US TO FIND.

OR THEY WON'T HAVE TO GO TO THE TROUBLE OF BURYING US.

NO SIGN OF THE UNION VESSEL.

EXCELLENT. INFORM CAPTAIN KRATOK THAT IT HAS BEEN DESTROYED.

HOW THE HELL DID THEY KNOW TO SCAN US WITH NEUTRON RADIATION?

I DON'T KNOW, BUT IT MEANS THAT WE CAN'T USE THAT CALIVON DEVICE AGAIN.

WE'VE GOT BIGGER PROBLEMS THAN THAT.

THEY'RE GOING TO NOTICE THERE'S NO DEBRIS.

AND THEN IT IS ONLY A MATTER OF TIME BEFORE THEY FIND US.

IF WE JUST HAD A FEW MINUTES TO GET OUT OF THE ASTEROID FIELD, WE MIGHT BE ABLE TO JUMP TO QUANTUM AND GET AWAY.

TUNNELING OUT OF THE CAVE WILL TAKE THREE POINT SEVEN MINUTES.

THIS ACTION WILL UNDOUBTEDLY DRAW THE ATTENTION OF THE KRILL SHIPS.

WAIT, I GOT AN IDEA. WE CAN USE THE CALIVON HOLOGRAPHIC GENERATOR.

OH, HEY BUDDY, DID YOU JUST MISS THE PART OF THE CONVERSATION WHERE WE TALKED ABOUT WHAT A CLUSTERFUCK THAT WAS?

YEAH, JOHN I DON'T THINK WE'RE GOING TO GET AWAY DISGUISED AS A KRILL SHIP.

NO, WE USE IT TO DISGUISE ANOTHER SHIP...

...AS THE ORVILLE.

WE DISGUISE THE TRANSPORT SHIP, AND PILOT IT BY REMOTE CONTROL. ITS ENGINES ARE MORE POWERFUL THAN A SHUTTLE'S SO IT'LL BE HARDER TO CATCH.

AND SINCE IT'S A ONE WAY TRIP, WE CAN RUN THEIR ENGINES AT MAXIMUM.

THAT MIGHT WORK.

THAT HAS TO WORK. GET ON IT. WE DON'T KNOW HOW LONG IT'S GOING TO TAKE THEM TO NOTICE THERE'S NO DEBRIS...

OUR SISTER SHIPS HAVE FAILED TO LOCATE THE UNION VESSEL.

THEY COULD NOT HAVE ESCAPED! THEY MUST BE IN THAT FIELD SOMEWHERE!

I HAVE NOTICED SOMETHING ON THE LARGE ASTEROID...

WHY DID YOU LOCK OUT YOUR SYSTEMS?

AVIS GUIDED US TO PROTECT OUR SHIP. WHAT DO YOU WANT WITH IT?

WE NEED IT AS A DISTRACTION TO ESCAPE KRILL SPACE.

THAT IS NO CONCERN OF OURS.

SO YOU'RE GOING TO SACRIFICE EVERYONE ABOARD THIS SHIP?

IT IS THE WILL OF AVIS.

BUT IF YOU FREE US, WE WILL DO OUR BEST TO CONVINCE OUR KRILL BROTHERS TO LET YOU RETURN HOME IN PEACE.

YOU DON'T SERIOUSLY--

CRSSSHHH

GRAYSON TO BRIDGE. BORTUS, WHAT THE HELL IS GOING--

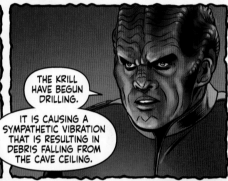

THE KRILL HAVE BEGUN DRILLING.

IT IS CAUSING A SYMPATHETIC VIBRATION THAT IS RESULTING IN DEBRIS FALLING FROM THE CAVE CEILING.

IN A CONFINED SPACE LIKE THIS, THAT COULD OVERLOAD A LOT OF OUR SYSTEMS.

JOHN, GET TO ENGINEERING, WE'VE GOT TO GET OUT OF HERE.

CRSSSHHH

WHAT HAPPENED?

THE SECURITY SYSTEM OVERLOADED.

I'LL GET HIS GUN.

THIS IS OUR CHANCE. WE'LL HIDE ABOARD OUR SHIP, AND WHEN OUR BRETHREN FINISH TUNNELING THROUGH, WE'LL ESCAPE.

COME ON.

WE MADE IT.

AVIS IS WITH US. RELEASE THE LOCKOUT, WE'LL START THE ENGINES.

I... DON'T THINK WE SHOULD LEAVE.

WHAT ARE YOU TALKING ABOUT?

THEY NEED THIS SHIP. WE CAN'T JUST LEAVE THEM TO DIE.

IT IS THE WILL OF AVIS.

UH, DARDEN, I THINK SHE'S RIGHT.

ME TOO. WE SHOULD HELP THEM.

NO!

I WON'T LET YOU! AHHH!

GUY WAS GETTING ON MY NERVES.

Moments later...

SIR, THE UNION VESSEL...

ALL SHIPS, PURSUE!

THEY TOOK THE BAIT.

LET'S GO. TAKE US TO QUANTUM AS SOON AS WE'VE CLEARED THE ASTEROID FIELD.

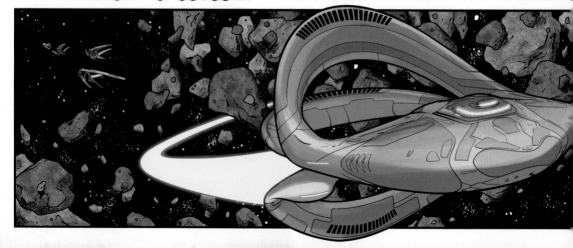

BING

COME IN.

HOPE I'M NOT BOTHERING YOU.

NO. THANK YOU FOR GETTING ME THESE QUARTERS.

YOU HELPED WHEN IT MATTERED. IT MEANT A LOT.

YEAH, EXCEPT NOW I HAVE NOTHING.

I THOUGHT THE ANKHANA GAVE ME AN IDENTITY. NOW THAT THAT'S GONE... I DON'T EVEN KNOW WHO I AM.

I GET THAT. I REALLY DO.

LITTLE WHILE AGO I WAS A LITTLE LOST. HAD TO FIGURE OUT WHO I WAS, GET MY LIFE ON A NEW TRACK.

HOW'D YOU DO IT?

TOOK A HELPING HAND FROM A FRIEND.